The New Pastor

Bethel Community Book
1

Sherman Cox

Connect with Sherman Cox

Twitter: @shermancox

Website: www.shermancox.com

Blog: www.shermancox.com/blog

Facebook: https://www.facebook.com/shermancox

Sign up for the author's New Releases mailing list:
http://www.shermancox.com/new-releases-club/

Table of Contents

Chapter 1 - Elliot

The 90 inch television dominated the small apartment's combination living/dining room. Elliot James, a 32 year old slender, but well-built African American man, lay on the couch as the television blared in the background. Elliot wore blue sweatpants with a number of holes peppered throughout them but concentrated in the knee.

His white t-shirt had multiple juice stains on it. The fingers of Elliot's right hand barely touched the television remote control. His head was turned to the left side as he snored while lying across the sofa. Next to Elliot was a large, half empty bag of barbecue potato chips so stale that they no longer had any crunch left in them. Half of the bag of chips was on the couch and the rest was still inside the bag. His left hand was in the bag. In front of him was a coffee table with an open can of soda sitting on it.

Jeremy Williams, Elliot's roommate, walked through the front door, saw Elliot lying there and yelled, "What the hell! I have people coming over and you messed up the living room." Jeremy yelled a few expletives and then shook Elliot as he said, "El…El…Get up El!"

Elliot jumped, which caused him to knock over the can of soda. At the same time the bag of chips were sent flying to the floor. The soda from the can spread out on the table and began dripping onto the floor.

"See? This is why I am through with you."

"Come on man, I was just about to clean up." Elliot said as he picked up the soda can and attempted to stop the growing flow of liquid with his hand.

"Why are you home?" Elliot asked. Elliot wasn't expecting Jeremy for at least a few more hours, which would have given him time to make the apartment presentable.

"I have Leslie coming over and I should have known you would be in here tearing my place up." Jeremy walked into the kitchen and then said, "For a brother who don't cook, I can't understand why the kitchen is always torn up. Why didn't you do the dishes?"

"I was gonna get to that, but you got home early."

Jeremy yelled from the kitchen again, "Elliot! Come on man, I told you not to touch that cake, it is for Leslie's family…"

"Oh, I'm sorry, I thought you said I could get just one slice." Elliot lied as he rushed into the kitchen to put a few plates into the dishwasher.

Jeremy kept looking in the refrigerator and said,

"Naw…No way, where is my punch?"

"You mean that Kool Aid that was in the pitcher?"

"You know what I mean. And you know that wasn't Kool Aid." Jeremy walked over to the sink, pushed Elliot out of the way, and began putting the plates into the dishwasher.

"I will be glad when you get up out of here. I sure hope your interview went well today…How did it go?" Jeremy asked as he began cleaning up the kitchen.

"You know what, I was thinking I could get a degree in Spanish Literature. There is always a need…"

Jeremy started laughing. "You got to be the most educated unemployed brother in the country. How many master's degrees do you need to sit on my couch and eat up my food? That's it. Leslie tells me I need to stop enabling your stupid behind. So let me tell you this, this is the last month I carry you."

"Huh? Carry me? I gave you 200 bucks last week."

Jeremy threw his hands up in the air and yelled, "Rent is 950 dollars and you gave me 200 bucks. And for the record that was at least 3 weeks ago." Jeremy laughed. "Remember when you said you would start paying half of the rent starting in March?"

"Yeah, but my job fell through and…"

"Your job always falls through El. You never work El. It is June and you haven't been on one job interview. We boys, but I can't carry your trifling behind anymore."

"OK, I will get you half this month man."

Jeremy stopped working and said, "I can't clean this place up. I will take Leslie and her folks out to that new Italian restaurant. Let me get me some Flavor O's and take a nap so I can be ready for them."

Elliot stopped cleaning up when Jeremy said he would take Leslie's family out.

Jeremy grabbed the box of Flavor O's from off the top of the refrigerator. He took a mixing bowl and turned the box upside down attempting to fill the bowl. Five or six pieces of cereal fell out of the box. Jeremy's light brown skin became beet red and he looked in the box. Jeremy laughed and said surprisingly softly, "Elliot, you ain't even been to get the groceries."

"Oh, I was going to go in a few minutes, I wasn't expecting you so…"

Jeremy composed himself and said, "Elliot, I am taking a nap, when I get up I expect the kitchen will be presentable and you will have purchased and put away the groceries. I gave you the money this morning El."

Jeremy started to walk towards his room. Elliot said to him, "I needed to…"

Jeremy put up his hand to signify he didn't want to talk and then walked into his bedroom. The door and the wall shook as he slammed the door.

Elliot realized he better get to the grocery store, but he also needed to look presentable if he was going to go out. He put on some slacks and put on a clean shirt. He found the grocery list, which was on the coffee table. It had a few stains on it from the can of soda.

"I was just about to go. Yelling at me, I was just about to do this. What's the matter with that brother?" Elliot said to himself under his breath so no one could hear. He grabbed the keys and went out and got into his old clunker of a car.

Elliot popped the hood and checked the oil levels in his car because it burned oil. He estimated that he could get to the grocery store and back without much of an issue. He hopped into the car and drove off.

Chapter 2 - Elliot

Elliot slowly drove over to the supermarket. Every Friday Jeremy expected him to do the grocery shopping and just about every Friday he missed it because he was either sleeping on the couch, working out at the gym, or playing ball with the college kids back at the university.

He knew why Jeremy was angry with him, but he also didn't like to be talked to like he was a child. It was especially true that he hated to be treated like a child when he was acting like a child. Elliot kept his eye on the heat indicator because his car was prone to overheating. He drove slowly to the grocery store and parked in the first open slot he could find.

Elliot walked into the supermarket on Harding and Bell Road. It was one of those super centers that was essentially a supermarket and a department store rolled up into one. He had a mission to get everything on the list. However, the two things he had to get most of all was milk. Elliot was happy that Jeremy didn't figure out that there was none.

In addition, Elliot had to get Jeremy's favorite

breakfast cereal the Flavor-Os. Elliot walked over to get the milk, gripping in his mind about how Jeremy was too old to be eating a children's breakfast cereal. He laughed at the thought of big high and mighty Jeremy bent over a bowl eating cereal with the kids. He grabbed a half gallon of milk and put it in the shopping cart.

He walked up and down every aisle, picked up all of the items on the list as well as a few other additions. He had to replace the soda pop and the potato chips that had gone flying. He also had to buy some cleaning materials to clean up the mess that he had made. He also needed a few school supplies. Might as well get it on Jeremy's dime rather than his own, Elliot thought.

He looked down on his list and saw that everything was now crossed out except the Flavor-Os. He knew that there was no way he was going to go home without them. So he began to walk towards them when he saw a very attractive African American woman wearing a slightly tight business suit walking down the aisle he was in. Elliot's eyes opened wider as he saw her walking toward him. Elliot pushed towards the woman, thinking that he could get the Flavor-Os after he got this woman's phone number.

He rushed down the aisle and turned and saw that the woman was in the breakfast cereal aisle. In addition, she was straining to reach a box barely out of her grasp.

Elliot followed the curves of her well-proportioned body with his eyes as she showed great determination in trying to get the cereal, but as she tried, only the tips of her fingers would touch the box.

The woman was only about 5 foot 6. Her body was slender. The business suit could not hide her feminine curves. She had rich and flowing dark brown hair that hung to her shoulders. Before Elliot could think, he rushed over to her side.

"Hello, I couldn't help but recognize that you are a little upset, do you need any help?"

She calmed down and looked into Elliot's eyes. Elliot couldn't help but notice her beautiful hazel eyes that had a dark brown ring around them. She smiled and it lit up the room.

"Oh, thanks, I am trying to reach that box of cereal up there, they always put it up so high."

Elliot smiled back at her and looked up and saw that she was reaching for a box of Flavor-Os. He then looked closer and saw that there was only one box of Flavor-Os up there. He looked at the tag and saw that they were on sale so they must have sold out very quickly.

Elliot's countenance immediately dropped. He was conflicted in that moment, and he didn't know what to do. Should he get the box and attempt to get the contact information of this beautiful woman that seems to have dropped into his lap? Of course that would mean that he would anger his roommate Jeremy once again. Maybe he would finally put him out of the house like he had been planning for so long.

Elliot then reasoned if he got the box, she would say thank you and be on her way, and he might not ever see her again. What if they go out and they don't hit it off? What if she blows him off? All of these thoughts went through his mind in a second and finally after processing the situation, Elliot went from single brother on the prowl to hungry brother chasing his last meal and took the box and threw it into his cart.

"What? I know you didn't just do that." The woman said to Elliot. "I know you didn't just take my Flavor-Os." She continued.

Elliot grabbed a box of Shredded Wheat which was right below it and threw it into the woman's cart and said, "This is just as good." And began to leave. He then turned around and asked, "Maybe we could..." He thought about asking her for her number and then thought better of it. And said, "Never mind." And then he rushed to the checkout line.

"No he didn't. No he didn't just take my Flavor-Os. This did not just happen." Elliot heard the woman say as he was rushing away.

Elliot turned around and the woman was standing there with her mouth open staring at Elliot. Elliot turned around and rushed to the checkout line. He wasn't particularly proud of what he had done, but he knew he didn't want to make Jeremy any angrier with him.

Elliot looked at his list and smiled, as he had now gotten everything on it. He stood in line and as always it seems like it was the slowest line. A few minutes later the attractive woman was checking out of the store. Elliot didn't want to look, but he couldn't help it. The woman gave him dirty looks every time he looked her way. When Elliot was finally checked out of the grocery store he rushed to his car to avoid seeing her any longer.

As Elliot was emptying the items from his cart and putting it all into his car the woman walked by and began putting her things in her trunk. She was parked right next to him. She wasn't saying anything, but the tension was very thick.

"I'm sorry, I just had to get that cereal." Elliot said.

"I know this guy didn't steal my cereal and now he is trying to make nice." The woman said while talking to the air.

Elliot figured that this confirmed to him that he had made the right decision. He wondered why she had to be so acidic.

Elliot got in his car while the woman was still putting things into her car. He then rolled down the window and said, "I'll be thinking of you while I'm eating."

Chapter 3 - Shereese

Shereese was very agitated as she sat in her apartment eating a bowl of shredded wheat and talking on the phone to her best friend Rachel Griffith.

"So I run into this nice looking brotha at the grocery store. I was trying to grab the Flavor-Os."

"You still eat that stuff? I ain't had any of that children's food in years."

"That ain't the point Rachel..."

"When you gonna start eating some grown folks cereal?"

"Can I finish the story?"

Rachel laughed.

"Anyway, I was trying to grab the cereal and this guy comes up to help me."

"So he reached up there and got it for you?"

"Naw girl, that fool took the Flavor-Os and put it right into his cart. What's the matter with men?" Shereese loudly hit her spoon on the bowl as it clanged.

"Oh no he didn't."

"Yes he did, then he had the nerve to put some

shredded wheat into my cart."

"I know you girl, did you go and take it out of his cart?"

Shereese laughed and said, "I was so shocked, I bought the shredded wheat and went home."

They both laughed.

"How are we supposed to date guys when so many are selfish little kids?" Shereese added.

"I don't know why you worried, you are dating Mr. Perfect. I bet you David would have given you your cereal." Rachel said while emphasizing the word David and perfect.

"Stop it." Shereese said smiling. "You know nobody's perfect."

"You are 30 years old and you are the senior accounting manager at a top accounting firm in Atlanta and you are about to be married to the most eligible bachelor in town, and you complaining about some Cheerios?" Rachel said.

"It's Flavor-Os. Thank you."

"I don't care if it is frosted mac and cheese, most of us wish we had what you have girl."

"Well, it ain't all peaches and cream. I am working 60 hours a week and then trying to get the books straight in my father's church. My father has been dead for 5 years and I am still tied to it like a ball and chain."

Shereese paused and then continued. "But when David gets this church in LA and I transfer to the LA office of Carlton-Mack, then you can envy me."

"I'm gonna miss you girl."

"Well David ain't got his church and I ain't got my ring, so until then, I will complain about my Flavor O's if that is all right with you."

They both laughed.

"I gotta let you go girl, those housewives are coming on. You gonna look at them too?" Rachel said.

"Naw girl, I don't look at that mess anymore, ever since they put off my girl."

"Well, I can't miss it, see ya."

They hung up.

Shereese chomped on the cereal and thought about the day. She just couldn't stop thinking about that nice looking guy who would take her cereal. Yes she was angry, but she also was slightly enamored when she remembered his voice. She thought he was going to ask her for her number and she wondered if she would have given it to him.

But then he showed himself to not be a knight in shining armor, but a selfish conniver just like all the other men who have been in her life.

Shereese finished the bowl of cereal and walked over to the television and turned on the housewives reality show that she had just said she wasn't gonna look at.

The phone then rang.

Shereese said to herself, "Saved by the bell." She then picked up the phone and said, "Hello."

"Shereese, how are you doing baby doll."

"Minister Harris, now I done told you I'm too old for you to be calling me that."

"I'm your godfather, and your daddy told me to take care of you when he crossed the river of Jordan, so I will call you my Baby Doll till I die. And you need to let Rev. Michael know that he better ask me for your hand..."

"Why are you talking about that, he hasn't asked me yet."

"I'm just letting you know, I love you like you are one of my own..."

"You know I love you too Pops."

"Why ain't you out anyway? Is that David Michael treating you right?"

"He's out preaching a revival. He said he was going to catch up with me tomorrow."

"Baby, will you get off that phone and get over here." Shereese heard a woman yell in the background.

"Is that momma Harris? You know she don't play that, you better get to her."

"I just wanted to say hey, and remind you early that we need you Monday morning to interview that new pastoral candidate. I sure hope he works out. We have a few interviews for the church secretary position as well."

"I can't make it, I have a meeting at work. I mean really, why do I have to even be there?" Shereese whined.

"Don't make me pull off my belt, you are gonna be there because I said you are gonna be there. This is your daddy's church and you need to be there. Besides, I don't really trust your momma…She is still trying to force your boyfriend David to take the church and make you first lady.

Shereese laughed, "She knows we are leaving as soon as David gets his L.A. church."

"Well, she is going to make it difficult for whoever comes as the new pastor so we are gonna need you to help run some interference."

"Mom will be all right once we leave, and really, why are we even looking for a pastor?"

"What are you talking about? We need a pastor."

"We have a pastor, why don't we just turn your title from 'interim' to 'senior pastor?'"

"Now you know I don't have the degree and the board ain't gonna go for that."

"Baby, you better get off that phone!" The lady in the background yelled.

"It's Shereese Hun." Minister Harris said.

Then the phone clicked over and a woman started talking. "Hey Shereese, tell my husband to get off this phone."

"Hey momma Harris." Shereese said.

"I think I gotta go. Love you baby girl…" Minister Harris said.

"Love you Pops." Shereese said as she hung up the phone.

Chapter 4: Elliot

On Sunday afternoon, Elliot's old clunker was spewing smoke into the atmosphere as he was driving to the mall. Jeremy had not been pleasant to be around since he blew up at Elliot on Friday.

That Sunday morning, Jeremy woke up and harped on Elliot's lack of job opportunities before he went to church. Elliot hadn't been in a church for a while and really didn't want to go to Jeremy's church and hear this all through the service. Plus Jeremy let Elliot know that he was going to bring Leslie's family home after church and that he best not be there.

Elliot decided to walk around a few stores and then catch a couple of movies at the Cineplex before heading back to the apartment later in the evening.

Elliot knew that it was entirely his fault and he recognized the need to find a job, but he just was trying to find the right job that fit his skill set. And he had to figure out what his skill set was. Whenever Elliot needed to think, he would go lounge around the mall and then catch a movie.

Elliot began walking around the mall. It was about noon so the church set hadn't gotten there yet. He saw some teenagers walking around and some elderly folks doing some power walks. As he walked, his mind went back to the events of the weekend. He thought about lazing around the house and how his life was quickly passing him by. He thought about the lack of direction that he has had in his life and his continual search for ease and laziness.

And then Elliot looked to the right and saw an elderly man and women hand in hand walking. Elliot's thoughts immediately went to whether he would find that one and what he would do after finding that one. Then inexplicably the woman at the grocery store came to mind. He wondered who she was and whether she could have been more if he hadn't been so stupid.

He then pushed those thoughts out of his mind and he began to think about Carman, the girl he was dating now. He knew that nothing was coming from it, and thinking about her didn't really alleviate the deep thoughts that began plaguing his mind. But then he began planning their next date, which caused him to forget about the deep thoughts that he didn't really want to address.

He walked towards the food court and saw one of his friends from the not too distant past. Elliot rushed over to his old friend Barry, who was dressed up in a suit.

"Barry O, it has been a long time. Man, you are

looking clean, boy?"

They shook hands.

"What up El, it has been a good while, yeah, I just got out of church. I go to Bethel on Wickshire. Minister Aaron is really dealing in that pulpit."

"Church?"

"I am trying to get my life together, I started attending Bethel and Minister Aaron really hooked me up."

"Church? Minister Aaron? Naw man, not you? What's gotten into you?" Elliot joked.

Barry laughed, "Yeah man, Church. I have been changed. Been going to church for a while. I found a job. My life is taking a turn for the better El."

Over to the right a young woman with one of those big church hats and a loud colored dress came over and hugged Barry.

"Hey El, this is my wife, Juanita. We are about to go hit the cafeteria before going to the Cineplex." He paused as Juanita shook his hand. "Juanita, this is my boy El. We were in school together...remember the brother I said had 5 degrees."

"Oh yeah, wow, Elliot." The woman said.

"It's 4 degrees." Elliot said.

"Wife? Dang has it been that long since I talked to you. Man, congratulations." Elliot continued.

Barry laughed and said, "Thanks man, I wanted to invite you, Jeremy, and the boys, but it was all of a sudden, we have to get to Chicago and we wanted

Minister Aaron to perform the ceremony, so we had a small wedding."

"Ahh don't worry bout that, I'm just happy for you man. But why do you have to leave?"

"Well, Juanita is starting an MBA in Chicago and I found a job up there. Life seems to come together when you are about business. By the way, did you ever find a job, I know you were looking?"

"Naw, I'm still looking." Elliot answered.

Juanita then said to Elliot, "I just turned in my notice at the church as their secretary. It is a lot of paperwork and stuff, but if you went to college with Barry, I bet you could do it. You ought to apply."

Barry laughed and said to Juanita, "This brother probably has a degree in paperwork amongst all those degrees. All he knows is how to shuffle paper."

Juanita pulled out a piece of paper and began writing on it. She said to Elliot, "Tell Minister Aaron you know me. They haven't even started advertising the job heavily yet. I think they only have a few applicants."

Elliot didn't like the idea of working as a secretary. He did have a number of degrees and felt that the job was beneath him.

He also didn't like the idea of working in a church. He had grown up in the church and had enough of church folks' messes. His uncle was a minister.

But he did like the idea of finally having a job, especially in light of the fact that Jeremy was close to being thru with him. He took the paper and smiled.

"Thanks you two."

"Hey why don't you hang out with us, we can catch up." Barry said to Elliot.

"Sure, I can tag along if you don't mind having a third wheel." Elliot said.

They talked in the cafeteria for an hour before heading over to the Cineplex to watch a movie.

Chapter 5 - Shereese

On Monday morning Shereese called Minister Aaron. "You know I been thinking."

"Uh Oh..." Minister Aaron answered.

"I am sure daddy would have wanted you to step in and take the church. Doesn't the words Pastor Harold Aaron have a nice ring to it?"

Minister Aaron exhaled loudly and said, "How many times do we have to go over this? To repeat, I grew up with your daddy. I knew your daddy longer than you knew your daddy, and he always believed in order. Which is why I am not the pastor. I never finished that degree and you know that."

He paused and then said, "Well, we have Pastor Carl K. Charles coming in for an interview today, I really hope we can get moving on this thing to get the church out of this holding pattern..."

"Poppi, that is why I called, he contacted David. He said that he wouldn't be coming. At least he wouldn't be coming soon. He still is interested in pastoring our church, but something happened at his church."

"Something happened at his church? Something like what?" Minister Aaron asked.

"I don't know, David didn't say."

"David. David. Why are all these people always talking about David? Why didn't he call me? Why is he calling David?"

"Well, many people think that David is the interim pastor. Perhaps he thought…"

Minister Aaron interrupted her, "He ain't the interim and he don't want to be the interim, he don't want to be the pastor, I am really getting sick of his game. What is he telling these other preachers?"

"I don't want to get between you and David, that's between you two, and really, I'm just the messenger."

Minister Aaron calmed down, "I ain't mad at you baby girl, I just am tired of David coming in here with information that I should have and not sharing it until it is good for him. If he wanted the pastor job, then why don't he just take the job so we can go on?"

"OK Poppi, did you get it out of your system yet?"

Minister Aaron laughed, "Did Reverend Charles want to reschedule?"

"No, he said that he would contact us when he is ready."

"He understands that we can't hold the position open for him?"

"Yes, he said that he would leave that in God's hands."

Minister Aaron chuckled and said, "Who am I kidding, the position has been open for 2 years and nobody wants it. It is a 150 member church. It is on the small side, but it is in Atlanta, Georgia. It has great potential."

"David would take it if he and I were not soon to move to L.A. and to the historic Barry Street Christian Church."

"You know our church ain't big enough for the great illustrious David Michael."

"Come on, is that fair?"

"If I weren't a minister, I would tell you more clearly what I think of your fiancé." Minister Aaron said. He then slowed down his voice and said, "Well, I...baby girl, I must say that I am glad we ain't getting him as pastor and I wish that you weren't getting him either."

"Now Poppi."

"I know, I know, I'll mind my own business." Minister Aaron then said "...maybe I can put my feelers out to find somebody that I haven't thought of until now to pastor the church. There is a young hotshot from the seminary that I am hearing about.

When are you coming in to work today?"

"Well I know I usually work a few hours on Monday, but since Reverend Charles has canceled, I figured I would just skip. I have some projects that I need to work on.

"OK, I will talk to you later baby girl."

Chapter 6 - Elliot

Elliot had on his best suit as he walked up to the church. He thought he looked more like an executive than a secretary. But he wanted the job and was willing to do whatever it took to get it. People always say dress for the job you want, and he always saw himself as moving on up.

He opened the front door and confidently walked into the church office on that Tuesday morning. He saw a man in a suit standing up, but answering the phone. The man looked a bit frazzled. Elliot walked up to the man and said, "Hello, I am here to apply for the job."

The man in the suit said, "Hold on, we really need to get a secretary in here. I wasn't expecting you, I thought you had canceled this meeting. My name is Minister Aaron." He shook Elliot's hand. "Forgive the mess, our secretary just quit on us and I have to hold it down until we hire another one."

Elliot was confused in that he had not had any contact with the church. He thought that Barry's wife must have called over to inform them he was coming. However,

Elliot couldn't remember her name so Elliot said, "Well the woman told me that the position was opening…"

"Yes, Yes, please sit down…well it has been open…I have seen your resume and I have a few questions for you."

Elliot knew he hadn't sent a resume over and wondered what resume Minister Aaron was looking at.

"I want to know what you think you can do in this position to help this church get to the next level." Minister Aaron said.

Elliot wasn't exactly sure what a secretary at the church would do. He had grown up in the church, but all he figured a secretary would do was answer some phone calls and set up some meetings. He knew that secretaries kept the calendar and all of these were very important functions, but he wondered how any of those things would take the church to the next level. He looked around and saw a lot of trash that needed throwing out and a lot of fixing and cleaning up to do and he keyed in on that.

"Well, I do believe that cleanliness is next to godliness and so we need to make sure that all the trash is placed where the trash should be placed." Elliot said.

"Trash? What trash?" Minister Aaron asked with a puzzled look on his face.

"Whether you are a church or not, I will do what the boss tells me to do to the trash. Some things need to be filed away over here and some over there, but I will make sure everything goes where everything should go."

A smile emerged on Minister Aaron's face.

Elliot continued, "And yes, some trash belongs in the can. Really, that would be my emphasis, at least at first. My emphasis would be to put the trash where the trash belongs and to put the good stuff in its proper location."

"Well I wouldn't refer to the people of God as trash, but maybe it is that kind of shock to the system that we need, we really are stagnant." Minister Aaron said.

"People of God? What are you talking about?" Elliot tried to interrupt.

"Well, if it were up to me, with your credentials I would hire you right now, but it is up to the search committee and of course you would have to give a trial sermon, can I schedule you for this Sunday?"

"Trial sermon?" Elliot asked with a real confused look on his face.

"Reverend Charles, I am not trying to insult you, but I know you didn't expect us to hire you as pastor of this church without even giving a trial sermon, I haven't even seen you before."

"Reverend Charles? Hold on, I think you might have made a mistake." Elliot said beginning to realize that Minister Aaron thought he was someone else.

"Come on Reverend, don't be like that, it is just our procedure. Assuming that the church selects you, we will start you at about $3,500 a month plus use of the parsonage." Minister Aaron continued. He then stopped and said, "Hold on, did you say a mistake?"

Elliot thought about $3500 a month and said, "Mistake, naw I misspoke, so you say you have scheduled me for this Sunday? Do you mind if I take a copy of my resume? I seem to have misplaced mine."

"No problem pastor Charles. Let me go make a copy right now." Minister Aaron had a big smile on his face as he shuffled over to the copy machine.

"So what happened to the previous pastor if I may ask?" Elliot asked.

"Oh Reverend Harris. My life long buddy. He died of a heart attack about three years ago." Minister Aaron said as he pushed the button on the copier.

"So why didn't the pastor just leave his son in charge or maybe the assistant? Isn't there another successor?"

"He doesn't have a child in the ministry, his daughter is a treasurer and the assistant doesn't want the job. It was so sudden. It wouldn't have mattered anyway, the pastor put in the bylaws that a duly elected pastor can't name his successor, but he can eliminate from contention any name he considers unacceptable. But you don't have to worry about that. I feel good about this Rev." Minister Aaron picked the resume up off the copier and walked over to Elliot and gave it to him. "I can't wait to hear your sermon Reverend." Minister Aaron continued.

Elliot took the resume and looked at it. He saw Reverend Carl K. Charles. He didn't know him, but obviously neither did Minister Aaron, who thought he was Reverend Charles.

Elliot smiled, "Thank you Minister for your kindness. I pray that the God of Abraham, Isaac, and Jacob send his blessings on you and this church." Elliot said in a preachers tone that he had heard while growing up in the church.

"All right now, you gonna get me to shouting up in here." Minister Aaron said.

Elliot began walking to the door.

"See you Sunday." Minister Aaron said.

Elliot smiled and continued walking to the door.

As Elliot walked out of the door he heard Minister Aaron saying, "Throw out the trash! That is exactly what this church needs."

Chapter 7: Elliot

"And God told me to tell ya that your breakthrough is just around the corner…" The well-dressed preacher yelled on the Christian Pulpit Network (CPN) television channel. Elliot usually changed the channel quickly when such preaching was on, but today he was searching to find African American preachers to study. He looked intently at the preacher.

Elliot was trying to get the content and the style of the preacher. Every time the preacher would move his arm, Elliot would pause the television and try to move his arm the same way. Then he would copy the gesture in unison with the preacher.

When the preacher pointed, he pointed. When the preacher raised his voice or took on a particular musical quality in his voice, Elliot would copy that too. Elliot was attempting to closely emulate the preacher's style.

Elliot also raised and lowered his voice in line with the preacher's example.

After Elliot noted some other point, he would pause the video again, jot his observation down in his notebook and then attempt to copy the preacher.

Elliot had filled thirty pages of his 100 page notebook in the few hours he had been studying the preachers.

"If God built it...then you better know it's gonna stand." The preacher said while pointing and leering at the congregation. Elliot paused the video, smiled and copied the gesture. He then began writing a few more notes in his pad. Elliot then un-paused the television so that the preacher could continue.

Jeremy walked into the front door of the apartment and walked over to the refrigerator to grab a can of soda.

The preacher started a verbal run and Elliot laughed in enjoyment as he wrote down some more notes into his notebook.

"Hey El, is that the Christian Television station?" Jeremy said as he took a gulp from the soda.

"Yep, CPN."

"Did you get the Lawd or something?" Jeremy laughed.

"Not only did I get the Lawd, I think I'm gonna finally accept my call to preach the gospel."

Jeremy stopped and stared at Elliot. He almost dropped the can of soda that was in his hand.

"Preaching? You?"

"Don't look so surprised, I grew up in the church, so when I went up in for that job interview they asked me to apply to be the pastor."

"Pastor? You? This sounds like another one of your

schemes that never pay off. Stop playing El."

Elliot laughed. "Oh yea of little faith, my trial sermon is this Sunday."

Jeremy laughed. "So you are going to preach a sermon this Sunday morning and you think they are going to give you a church?"

"Yep, and it is gonna pay off this time to the order of $3,500 bucks a month. I am going to do whatever I need to do to get that money."

"$3,500 dollars a month. Now I know you ain't gonna be able to pull this one off." Jeremy shook his head while laughing.

"If God closes one door, all you have to do is go on through that open one." Elliot said in a preacher's voice.

"What you don't remember is that one of my undergraduate degrees is in theater. And I played a black preacher in one of my most successful roles." Elliot continued.

"Successful roles? Did the first graders at the school cafeteria give you a standing ovation or something?" Jeremy laughed.

"You joking, but all I have to do is throw in some clichés about planting your seed and God bringing a harvest and then start shouting about God making a way out of no way. Add in a whoop at the end, and those Negroes will be swinging from the rafters. I know church folk. That's one thing I do know."

"You know church folk? Man you ain't been to church

in years. I been trying to get you to come with me and my girl and you always got an excuse. When is the last time you have even been to church?"

"It don't matter, it's like riding a bike. I grew up in the church. My Uncle Leon is a minister. He told me that I was called, and you know what, I believe him. The Lawd works in mysterious ways."

"Uncle Leon? I remember that guy, didn't you call him your crazy uncle?"

"Come on man, that's beside the point my brotha, I know what church folks want. Anyway, I have been looking at Christian television all day and it is just like I said, church folks are just looking for a reason to shout. I can play the game like anybody else."

"Whatever, you just be ready to pay the rent at the end of the month or I'm gonna have to put you out." Jeremy said.

"I won't need...this place..." Elliot started preaching while pointing downward. "You see, God has provided a better place." He pointed forward as he continued preaching.

"What are you talking about?"

Elliot began speaking normally again. "The job includes a parsonage, so if I get this job, I will be moving out man."

"You mean you finally gonna get up out of here? Now I feel like shouting, God is good...all the time..." Jeremy said.

Elliot rolled his eyes and then started preaching. "You are just like them haters. Always standing in the way. But God told me to tell ya not to worry bout the haters in your path. What God has for you is for you. God got me a new job…a new car…a new house…Come on give the Lord a hand-clap of praise." Elliot preached at Jeremy.

"They better give you a new car. I doubt they want to see their new pastor driving what you be driving." Jeremy said.

"Just leave me alone, I got work to do. I ain't got time to be playing. Let me practice my sermon." Elliot said.

Jeremy walked away smiling. Elliot began practicing his sermon. "Touch your neighbor and say, neighbor…"

Chapter 8 - Shereese

Shereese had learned to love being in church on Sunday morning. It had not always been that way. "If the Lord can give you 24 hours a day, then the least you can do is give him 1 hour on Sunday." Her father, the founding pastor, used to say. Shereese wondered which church only met for an hour, and she wanted to join it.

While she had all of the drawbacks of being a pastor's kid like all the other children of clergy, she also had a few perks that few members had.

You always got your food first during potlucks. You always had a seat. Sure they talked about you behind your back and held you up to an impossible standard, but being treated like royalty did have its perks and now Shereese was soon to marry a preacher. From pastor's kid to first lady. Her father had prophesied as much.

When Shereese was a child, her father used to tell her that one day she would be the first lady of a church. Shereese never wanted it, and actually ran from it, but now she was very close to being engaged to a preacher and would soon walk into her father's prophecy.

At church the people always seemed to fall over her as the founding pastor's daughter. Today was no different. She strode in with David Michael. David was a tall very attractive man. Shereese could feel the envy of the other women as she walked in with him. She would never admit it, but she actually enjoyed seeing this.

Shereese really didn't want to leave the church her father founded. In addition, she didn't really want to leave Atlanta, but she was willing to follow David. She had to admit that he was a little conceited and a bit hard headed, but she loved him and she believed he loved her. They made a very striking couple.

"Baby girl." Minister Aaron said as he hugged her.

"Poppi." Shereese said in response.

David smiled politely in a way that only barely hid his contempt and said, "Minister Aaron it is good to see you this Sunday morning." He lied.

Minister Aaron appeared to fight a frown and put his hand out to shake David's hand. "Reverend." He said to David.

"What's this I hear about a trial sermon going on today?" David asked.

"Yes Reverend Charles is going to preach."

"Reverend Charles, he told me he was not going to come here anytime soon. In fact, he said he was gonna be unreachable for a few months."

"Well maybe the interim pastor knows more than you

know." Minister Aaron said.

"I'm just telling you what he told me. I don't know him. I have never met or seen the man. I'm just telling you what he told me."

"Why is he telling you anything, why didn't you send him to me, I am tired of you undercutting my position David."

"Minister Harold Aaron, I wish you would call me Reverend David Michael in public."

"Reverend David Michael...Ok Reverend. And I expect you to treat the interim pastor like he is the pastor."

"Fine..."

"At any rate, he is here and he is going to preach."

"Where is he?"

"In the pastor's study."

"I want to go meet the man that wants to be the pastor." David said to Shereese.

The three began walking to the pastor's study.

"Minister Aaron, I didn't mean to undercut your position, it is just that the other preachers assume that I am the interim, it is not my fault."

"They assume and you don't correct them. Whatever, you may have Shereese fooled, you may even have most of the church fooled, but I got you pegged, and let me tell you this, you better not hurt this girl or I'm gonna hurt you." Minister Aaron pointed at Shereese.

"Poppi." Shereese said as they walked into the back

room.

Shereese saw the man and immediately recognized his attractiveness, but also couldn't shake the feeling that she had met him before.

"Reverend Charles." Minister Aaron said.

The man didn't move.

"Reverend Charles." Minister Aaron said louder.

Still no movement.

"Reverend Charles." Minister Aaron said almost yelling.

"Oh um, you mean me, oh, yes. Yes, Reverend." The man jumped up and looked around.

"That's minister." Minister Aaron said.

"Of course."

"I just brought in a couple people for you to meet. This is Reverend David Michael, the assistant pastor, and the daughter of our founder, Ms. Shereese Harris."

"Hello Reverend Charles, You look a lot younger than you sound on the phone." David said while reaching to shake the man's hand.

"I get that a lot."

"Well, what should we call you?"

"I just go by El."

"El?"

"You know short for Elliot."

"Elliot?"

"I thought your name was Carl K. Charles."

"Um…err. Elliot is my nickname."

"How did you get a nickname like Elliot?" David asked.

"Stop interrogating the man." Shereese said. "If the man wants to be called El, then call him El."

Shereese walked up to him and shook his hand and said. "Nice to meet you Reverend El."

"The only name that matters is "reverend." Minister Aaron said.

Eliot looked at Shereese and asked her, "Have we met before?"

"I can't help but think the same thing. Maybe at a church meeting or something." Shereese responded.

They both laughed awkwardly.

"Well I am sure the Reverend has some pressing matters so we will leave you right now." David said as he grabbed Shereese and rushed her out the room leaving Minister Aaron and Eliot in the room together.

While David and Shereese were out in the hall, David said to Shereese. "I can't believe you were flirting with that guy. I was standing right there."

"Flirting, what are you talking about?"

"I know flirting when I see it. Talking bout 'Have we met before?' What are you doing?"

"I don't know what you are talking about, I think I have met him before."

"Why you gotta be flirting like you are more than friends…I hate it when you do that."

"The only flirting that happened was in your mind."

David smiled as a member walked by.

"I think you should find a seat." David said to Shereese.

"Good, because I am looking forward to a sermon from my dear friend Reverend Eliot." Shereese said in an attempt to irritate David.

"See...Don't start." David said as Shereese walked away into the sanctuary to find a seat.

Chapter 9- Elliot

The scent from Shereese's perfume was still floating in the air as Elliot thought about his first encounter with Shereese at the grocery store fighting for the cereal.

Shereese appeared to not remember Elliot, but Elliot remembered immediately how attracted he was to her. He set aside his sermon in his mind for a moment and thought he might get some information out of Minister Aaron who was still in the room with him.

An usher rushed into the room with a mug of tea on a tray.

"You wanted this, reverend?" The elderly usher said while smiling.

"Thank you sister." Elliot said to the woman as she left the room.

Elliot took a drink of the tea and then thought he would try to find out some information about Shereese.

"Minister Aaron, that beautiful woman, you said her name was Sister Shereese Harris?"

"Yes...Yes...that is our late pastor's daughter. She is very attractive, isn't she?"

"Yes Minister, she is, but it appears Reverend Michael and her are an item."

Minister Aaron's face changed like he smelled something bad. "That is her no good boyfriend. I sure wish she could find a good man and not that kind of...I don't mean to be disrespectful, but some folks are just like you said, worthy of taking out in the trash."

"So how long have they dated?" Elliot asked.

Minister Aaron paused for a moment and then his eyes widened as if he figured something out. "Yes, yes. It has been a couple of years, but that doesn't matter, sometimes God has something for you, and what God has for you is for you." Minister Aaron said while emphasizing the word "you."

"Now what are you implying Minister?"

"Now this makes a lot of sense to me. After service I want you to come over to my house for dinner. Yes, this makes a lot of sense to me."

"I ain't come here to cause no trouble." Elliot said.

"You just leave it to me."

"Well hold on, what is the matter with Reverend Michael?" Elliot interrupted.

"With your experience, you know that the ministry brings a wide variety of people."

"Um...hmm..." Elliot said

"In the black church the pastor can be held in high esteem if he is loved by the people. And some people are attracted to the power and prestige that such a position brings you."

"So, he in it for the power?" Elliot asked.

"Well, I can't really say that, but I can say that something about him just don't sit right with me."

"Well certainly there are some people who come into the ministry for good reasons." Elliot interrupted.

"Of course, yes, yes, there are many great men in ministry. Shereese's daddy was a great man in the ministry. This church is a monument to his love for God and God's people. All I'm saying is that some people are attracted to the power."

"And the money." Elliot said under his breath.

"Well, it ain't a lot of money for what we expect the pastor to do. I mean when you become the pastor you will be expected to keep the church running as well as be a public minister in the community. This church has always been at the forefront of civil rights as well as social justice issues. You may even be asked to be on a number of boards."

"But is all of that necessary? I mean we must put the Lord's work first." Elliot said as he began to catch a glimpse of how big a job he was undertaking.

"Lord's work? All of that is the Lord's work. You gonna do more than preach, bury, and baptize if you gonna be an effective pastor in this church. Is that going to be a problem?"

"No...No...calm down Minister. I just was wondering if the money was going to be enough for all of that work."

"The money is what I told you, you don't need money do you?" Minister Aaron looked at Elliot.

"No Minister. So Reverend Michael is about power acquisition?" Elliot said trying to change the subject.

Minister Aaron smiled, "Well, like I said, some people are attracted to power and prestige but some folks are attracted to the idea of helping somebody.

"I can guess which group you think Reverend Michael is in." Elliot said.

"I don't want to sway you in your thinking about him, really I probably have said too much." Minister Aaron said.

"No…No…I think I need to know this."

"You get to know him. You'll figure out very quickly where he is coming from." Minister Aaron said.

Elliot smiled and took his Bible and began thinking about how this conversation might be a good sermon illustration, after he changed the names, when a final thought hit him.

He took a sip of the still piping hot tea and sat it down on the table.

"I have one more question, Minister." Elliot asked as he opened his Bible and felt the leather on his fingers.

"Sure go ahead, but we don't have much time left; we need to get in there."

"Which group do you think I am in?"

"Why do I think you are in the ministry? Is that what

48

you are asking?"

"We shall see...we shall see. Now come on, you have to make your entrance."

"My entrance?"

"Yes, at this church the pastor enters from the rear into the sanctuary."

"I ain't the pastor yet."

"Let's hope that changes soon." Minister Aaron said. "Now come on Reverend. And don't you let nobody invite you to dinner, you coming over to my place."

Chapter 10 - Shereese

The building that could hold about 400 comfortably was about half full. Four singers were leading the praise team. It was now the hymn portion of the praise and worship period. Shereese loved those old hymns as much as the mothers of the church who were now all standing and clapping. She stood with them. Only a few members were seated and all sang.

"Down at the cross where my savior died, Down where from cleansing from sin I cried, there to my heart was the blood applied, glory to His name." The singers led and the worshipers were singing to God's glory.

The ministers were standing as well. Minister Harold Aaron was standing to the right and Elder David Michael was on the left. The new minister who wanted to be called El stood in the middle.

The congregation didn't want to stop singing as the spirit moved throughout the entire congregation that Sunday morning.

The praise team continued to lead the church in a few more old hymns. They finished with a very spiritual rendering of "Holy, Holy, Holy."

Minister Aaron, waited a few minutes to allow the spirit to touch a few more in the congregation. He then approached the microphone as one could hear a few voices in the back ground, "Yes Lord." And someone clapped loudly.

Minister Aaron began, "Praise Him." And the congregation erupted in applause. "Y'all don't hear me, Praise Him!" Folks in the congregation started waiving their hands and you could hear some people saying things like, "Preach it Doc."

"Y'all gonna get me started." He said while laughing. "But no, I have a big surprise for you. Today we are blessed to have the Reverend Doctor Carl K. Charles. He is a pastor, the senior pastor of Jericho Hope Community in Los Angeles. That church has grown over 200 percent over the last few years. He is a preacher, he has taught and ordained ministers throughout the country..."

Shereese looked at the man again. She just couldn't get rid of the feeling that she knew him or at least had seen him before.

Minister Aaron continued to sing the praises of Carl K. Charles as Shereese attempted to figure out how she knew him. One thing Shereese knew was that Minister Aaron was trying very hard to get the church to accept this guy as the next pastor. She stared at him sitting behind the podium. He looked a little young to have done all that Minister Aaron claimed he had done.

"...And now this man is applying to become out next pastor. Now I could go on for hours, but you need to hear him. In fact you very much want to hear him. My sisters and brothers, I present to you, the Reverend Doctor Carl K. Charles."

Then the man walked up from and shook hands with Minister Aaron. Shereese guessed that he was about her age and he was already a doctor and had grown another church. She couldn't help but think he was a very attractive man, but that wasn't why she couldn't get him out of her mind. Then he began to speak.

"I want to thank you Minister Aaron and the whole church family for the love you have shown me." He began.

"Someone asked me this morning if I needed something. I said no, everything I have asked for, someone gave it to me. Your ushers and deacons are so nice." He continued.

"I think if I asked them for milk or food or even a bowl of cereal you would have it in the back somewhere." The preacher said.

That's when it hit her. She remembered completely that the preacher, this guy that wants to be called El, was the same guy who had stolen her Flavor-o's cereal from her.

She was happy that she had figured it out and almost

jumped, but then she immediately got angry.

The same guy that stole my cereal thinks he is going to take my father's church? She said to herself.

***

Elliot then said, "I could go on and on, but God has a message today. But one final word of introduction I just have to say it that it is a marvelous blessing to be here at this time. God is certainly good."

"All the time." The congregation responded.

"Now I talked briefly to Minister Aaron who told me that this church was looking for leadership. I began thinking about great leaders. I thought about Donald Trump."

"Yes." Someone shouted.

"I thought about Steve Jobs...I thought about Martin Luther King. I even thought about Phil Jackson. Yes I thought about leaders."

"Yes sir." Someone else shouted.

"But I want you to know, when I think about leading, and I think about leadership, I have to think about Jesus."

A bunch of folks shouted. Elliot looked throughout the audience and saw the stunningly attractive Shereese that he now knew was the woman he had stolen the cereal from. And she was looking back at him with a hard and angry look. He wondered if she remembered him.

"Now, sometimes we think about Jesus as a little babe in Bethlehem. You know the quiet and meek baby Jesus." Elliot said while looking at Minister Aaron who was beaming from ear to ear.

"That's right Doc." Someone said in the audience.

"And that is some of Jesus." Elliot paused for effect like he saw some of the preachers on TV do. Then Elliot yelled, "But that ain't All of Jesus."

"Uh Huh." A woman said.

"You see when I lead, I understand that Jesus includes the babe in Bethlehem, but sometimes you gotta become the man who threw out the money changers."

"That's right." Someone else shouted.

"I was thinking about calling this sermon Jesus the head janitor. You know how he takes out the garbage."

Minister Aaron said, "Yes sir."

"But then I remembered that Jesus doesn't just throw out the garbage, you see Jesus takes old stuff and turns it into something new. Can I get a witness?"

"Yes…" Someone yelled.

"So I'm gonna talk about Jesus not as the janitor, but as the re-cycler."

"Come on now." Someone shouted.

He went straight into his first point. The people were particularly enjoying his sermon, but every time he looked at Shereese she had an "I know you ain't right" look on her face.

He decided to worry about what she knew later and

just preach the best sermon he could preach. Anyway, Elliot knew that the sermon was going well by the response of the people.

Elliot had pieced together four or five television sermons almost seamlessly. He was even putting his theatrical training to good use.

Elliot got to his final point. "Now as I take my seat, in case you don't know, Heaven is just a temporary spot for the people of God, for Revelations tells us that the New Jerusalem is going to come back to this Earth. I'm still talking about Jesus the recycler. Jesus is gonna take this old Earth and make it into something new. You see John said, "I see a new Heaven and a new Earth." That ain't that surprising. Remember in Revelations 21:5 we are told that God is gonna make all things new. Get that, not new things, but things new."

"All right now." Someone shouted.

The ministers on the platform then stood up in support of the preacher as he began to bring the sermon to a close.

"God has plans for this church, and it is not new things, it is things new." Elliot continued.

"Preach Boy…Preach." Someone shouted.

"God has plans for your life, and it is not new things, it is things new."

"All right now."

"Today, it is time to stop looking for new things, and start looking for things new."

"When I look at that organ, I don't see replacing that organ, I see making that organ new. When I see this choir. God ain't gonna replace that choir, God is gonna make that same choir new. I wish I had a witness."

They were standing now as the church members really were feeling the message. Elliot could even feel it as he had left his sermon notes and was preaching without their benefit now.

"Today, I just say to you, look up and know that God is fixing to do something, and it ain't making new things...naw, it is making things new. Today, come with me and we can make things new. Stand with me today, and we can make things new. Today, let's do it, I ain't talking about making new things, I am talking about making things new." Then like he had seen some preachers do, he just sat down abruptly as the people continued shouting and praising God.

Reverend Michael looked at Elliot suspiciously. Minister Aaron shook his hand almost violently. And Elliot took a quick glance at Shereese and she was still looking at him with that hard knowing look.

Chapter 11 - Shereese

After church Rachel Griffith and Shereese were talking while sitting at the couch at Shereese's apartment.

"That brother sure threw down this morning. What's his name? Reverend Charles?" Rachel said.

"Yeah, he was all-right."

"All-right? We ain't heard preaching like that since your father was in good form. He could even give David a run for his money." Rachel said while laughing.

"Yeah, well. There is something I gotta tell you about the new pastor."

"And that brother is fine too. Is he married?" Rachel continued without acknowledging Rachel's comment.

"Would you be quiet and let me speak. I know that preacher."

"You know him?" Rachel asked.

"Yeah, remember that brother who stole my Flavor-O's at the store?" Shereese said.

"You talking about the guy who took your cereal and gave you that shredded wheat?"

"Yeah, well that preacher is that guy." Shereese said.

Rachel laughed.

"It's not funny." Shereese said.

"That is not the guy."

"Oh it's him. And I can tell he knew."

"How could it be him, he is a preacher from the west coast or something."

"I don't know how it could be, but I do know that is the man."

"Well, he can preach." Rachel said. "You probably caught him on a bad day."

"Bad day or good day, how is a minister gonna treat somebody like that?"

"Now come on Shereese, you of all people being a pastor's kid know that even at their best sometimes preachers ain't all they should be."

"You don't understand." Shereese protested.

"So what, you ain't gonna vote for him?"

"I can't in good conscious vote for a man who…" Shereese began.

"You ain't right Shereese. This preacher is the best preacher we have seen in a while and he actually wants to come to this church. You are about to leave and you want to leave us without a leader. Would your father want that?"

"My father wouldn't want a man who runs over his members to be the pastor either."

"You ain't right, give the man a chance." Rachel said.

At that point the front door opened and David walked

in.

"Is my food ready, baby?" David asked Shereese.

"Your girl here is trippin." Rachel said to David.

"What are you talking about?"

"She don't like the preacher and it looks like she gonna vote against him being pastor."

"I didn't say I was gonna vote against him, I just don't think he may be the best fit." Shereese said.

"Well, later today is the vote and I am not that sure if I like the guy either." David said.

"Am I losing my mind? What is the matter with you two?"

"Well David thinks I like the guy." Shereese said.

"I know what I saw, you were falling over yourself when you met him. But that ain't my problem. His sermon was without content, he was just riling up the people about nothing." David said.

"And what did you do in that last sermon. If I remember correctly you worked 'Mary had a little lamb' into your sermon." Rachel said.

"Is she staying for dinner?" David asked Shereese ignoring Rachel.

"No I'm leaving, but you two need to get it together because both of you know he is right for the job. They need to have the whole church vote..." Rachel said.

"Interim pastors are voted on by the committee, full pastors are voted on by the congregation." Shereese said.

"How about this. Let God's will be done. So you can

go now." David said.

Rachel picked up her purse and began walking to the door. "I love you too David." She said mockingly.

"You have a good rest of the day Sister Griffith." David said as Rachel left.

"Why do you two always have to fight?" Shereese asked.

"That's on your girl. But I want to know what turned you from Reverend Charles?"

Shereese didn't feel it best to get into why she was against the new preacher so she simply said, "You know for the same reason you are against him. His sermon seemed a bit empty."

David smiled and asked, "So what's for dinner?"

Shereese walked over to the kitchen and pulled a few items out of the refrigerator and said, "Just something I threw together, we have to get back to the church for the committee vote."

They sat down and warmed their food in the microwave before eating quickly so that they could get back to the church.

***

Minister Aaron chaired the committee vote. Shereese and David were seated next to each other and the head Deacon Bruce Miller. An elderly, overweight, and bald haired man. He had been a member of the church since its founding and had actually laid the bricks at the church.

Seated next to Bruce was Sarah Harris, the founder's wife. She was a regal woman though in her early fifties she still could turn the heads of some men in their twenties. Technically she was still the first lady of the church. She didn't do much in the church anymore, but she wanted to be at this meeting to vote in her husband's successor.

The treasurer was the final person on the committee. Tanya Ward a pretty woman in her early thirty's with an average build. Tanya took over the duties when Shereese no longer could do the job due to other work obligations.

"OK, we have two things to discuss. First, I think we all heard Pastor Charles preach this morning. I say we put it up for a vote to make him the interim pastor with the understanding that the congregation vote on making him full pastor in a few months."

"Hold up Minister" David interrupted. "We need to discuss this."

"What's to discuss? He wants to be pastor, he can preach, he has an impeccable resume." Tanya said.

"David, what's your problem? You don't want nobody else to get no glory?" Bruce Miller the elderly deacon boomed.

"Now come on you know me better than that." David said.

"OK, let's let everybody talk on the subject. I'll begin.

I liked him from the day he showed up in my office. I think we know enough about him to give him a chance to pastor the church. One thing we do know is he can preach. I vote yes." Minister Aaron said.

"I vote yes, he is young. He is vibrant. He seems to be able to talk the voice of the streets. He can take us into a new direction." Tanya said.

"I vote no. His sermon was weak and full of platitudes. Do you want a solid Biblical preacher or do you want a guy who is just spouting nonsense?" David said.

"I have to agree with David. I vote no as well for the same reason."

"OK, the vote is 2 to 2. What say you Deacon Miller?" Minister Aaron asked.

"This is perhaps the biggest decision we have ever had in this church since we lost our founder. I will vote however the first lady votes. Lady Harris, how do you vote?" Bruce said while looking at Sarah Harris.

"I understand the fear and apprehension of moving into a new direction. I sometimes wonder if I would be willing to step down from this place as first lady. I greatly desired David to take over the post and make my daughter first lady, but that is not to be."

Minister Aaron and Bruce Miller frowned.

"But I will say that his sermon was powerful. It reminded me of one of your father's greatest sermons." She looked at Shereese.

"I think it is time to move on and God has given us the man that should take over this church. I vote yes." Lady Harris said.

"Hold on, just wait..." David tried to interrupt.

"Well then I vote yes as well." Bruce said.

"Then Pastor Charles will be the interim pastor of the church. I thank you all. I will let him know." Minister Aaron said.

David shrunk into his chair.

"Now a new opportunity for ministry has opened up. The mayor has talked about a program to help the community. He calls it Operation Reach Back. This program will help at risk youth to get a solid foundation. I need to put two people on the committee. I would do it, but I can't do it. Now I am sure that Pastor Charles will be the first name on the committee, but we need someone else. There is a sizable time commitment, but it will help both the church and the community." Minister Aaron said.

"How about David?" Lady Harris said.

"No, I actually can't take on any responsibilities for the next few months, my calendar is full." David quickly said.

"Of course, why let real ministry interfere with your preaching calendar." Bruce said.

"Well, I actually had Shereese in mind. One of the sponsors is your company and you handled yourself very well the last time we had such a program." Minister

Aaron said.

"I don't know if I like that. What about Tanya, can she do it?" David said.

"Treasury work is too much to handle, it's either you or Shereese. So unless you are volunteering, I think we will have Shereese do it." Minister Aaron said.

"Can you do it?" Minister Aaron asked Shereese.

Shereese had a little bit of time so she could do it. While she was not too keen on working with the new pastor she did want to help the kids and do some real ministry.

"Yeah I can do it." Shereese said.

David frowned at her.

Minister Aaron then took a vote that made Shereese and the new pastor the church's representatives on the Mayor's endeavor.

Chapter 12 - Shereese

Shereese sat in her home at the dining room table eating a bowl of cereal instead of cooking a meal. David was out of town doing a week long revival. Shereese didn't do much cooking when David was on the road.

She put a spoon full of Flavor-Os in her mouth as the phone rang. She looked at her phone and it said, "Elliot James." She didn't know who Elliot James was and thought about ignoring the call.

But the phone kept ringing, she answered it before it went to the cell phone answering service.

"Hello?"

"Sister Harris, it is so good to talk to you. I am not bothering you, am I?" The voice on the other end said.

Shereese looked confused and said, "Um, No. But who is this?"

"It is Reverend Charles, Minister Aaron said I needed to talk to you about the homeless shelter work that is..."

"Reverend Charles, um hmm." Shereese interrupted.

"Yes, Reverend Charles, and we need to talk about..."

"Oh yes, we need to talk. What kind of minister takes

cereal from one of his members?"

"Well, I don't think I know what you are talking about." Elliot said.

"Oh you know what I'm talking about. You know full well, what I'm talking about. I saw you, you might as well not lie about it. I saw you, and I remember you." Shereese said.

"Oh, I think I might remember now." Elliot said.

"I knew it, I knew it was you."

"I uh…You know it was a rough week and I…"

"You what? You thought your rough week defends your desire to jack me for my Flavor-Os?" Shereese said angrily.

"Sister Harris, I realize I disappointed you."

"You betrayed your ministry."

"Well, I uh, think you are taking this a little far."

"You betrayed the Lord and you betrayed your ministry."

"Sister Harris."

"And, I just wonder…"

"Sister Harris." Elliot interrupted.

"What do you want?" Shereese said angrily.

"Minister Aaron told me that since I am the new pastor…"

"Interim pastor…" Shereese interrupted.

Elliot continued, "…Interim pastor. Since I am the new interim pastor, I should talk to you about hitting the ground running and then moving forward. He then said to speak specifically about this homeless shelter project."

"Well, I don't know why Minister Aaron wants you to talk to me. You are only an interim pastor. I don't know why I should talk to you about hitting the ground running or moving forward. You are a pastor, you know what to do."

"Uh huh." Elliot said.

"As for the homeless shelter project, you just show up, say a word, and leave, we will take care of all the real work. I assume you don't want to get your hands dirty."

"And why would you assume that?" Elliot said.

"I'm just going from past experience."

"Hold on." Elliot said.

"Again, what do you want?" Shereese said with her best 'sista-girl' accent.

"What do I have to do to smooth over this cereal thing?" Elliot asked.

It then hit Shereese that she was kind of being a little petty. She knew she didn't trust the guy.

She had his resume sitting on the dining room table. She pulled it out and saw that he had a lot of successful ministry. She just couldn't toss away all that ministry without giving him a chance.

She calmed down and said, "OK, just meet me at the church tomorrow."

"Why thank you Sister Harris. Can I call you Shereese?" Elliot asked.

"I'll call you Reverend Charles and you will call me

Sister Harris." Shereese said.

"That sounds fine. I will see you tomorrow Sister Harris."

"Bye, Reverend Charles."

Shereese let out an audible yell. "Why do I have to work with this guy?" Shereese yelled loudly.

Her phone buzzed again. She looked and saw Elliot James again. She remembered that that was the phone that Reverend Charles was using.

"Now who is this Elliot James character?"

"Elliot James? Oh, uh."

Shereese continued, "Did you steal his phone like you stole my cereal?" Shereese said into the phone."

"Sister Harris, I apologize for that, I wish I could take it back, I really needed that cereal, but it was no excuse."

"Ok pastor, then who is Elliot James?"

"He is my nephew, he let me use his phone until I got my own."

"And why are you calling me back?"

"I can't do it tomorrow, can you meet me the day after…"

"OK, here we go…"

"No, I have a prior ministry engagement."

"OK, the day after, but you are not winning me over to your side by dropping out of this appointment."

"Just give me a chance. If you give me a chance, I will show you that God has a work for me to do at this church."

"Whatever..." Shereese said. She had heard it all before, preachers who don't do any real work of ministry because they are too busy looking for the limelight.

For a moment she thought that she had been a bit too hard on him, but now him breaking their appointment and then claiming that it was due to a ministry concern, really set her off.

"Don't be like that." Elliot said.

"I will see you on the day after tomorrow. Bye Pastor."

"I thank..."

Shereese clicked the phone to hang up on him mid-sentence.

This guy ain't gonna be pastor for long anyway, and if he is, at least I won't be here to have to deal with him. She thought.

She went back to her Flavor-Os and took a bite. Each bite brought back into her mind the stolen box from the pastor.

She picked up Reverend Charles' resume and balled it up and tossed it into the trash. She then took another piece of paper that had on it information regarding a youth ministry program that she was trying to institute.

Then she sat it aside and thought she might read up on the homeless program because it had undergone some modification since the last time she was working in it regularly.

She took another bite of cereal and read the paper.

Chapter 13 - Elliot

"Pastor Charles. I don't know if anybody told you, but we expect you to be at the church for at least four hours every weekday." Minister Aaron said on the phone as Elliot sat on the couch eating a bowl of Flavor-Os.

"Oh, Minister, I didn't..." Elliot began to say.

"No harm, no foul, but you should know that there are some people who are not really supportive of your appointment."

"Who you tellin?" Elliot said, agreeing with the sentiment.

Minister Aaron laughed, "Oh so someone has already let you know?"

"Well, Reverend David Michael seems to not like me much at all, and his fiancé Shereese, she seems to not like me much either."

"Well, I wouldn't worry too much about Reverend Michael. He only cares about himself. I am not sure why Shereese is upset with you though. Maybe I can talk to her and kind of smooth things over."

"No...No...No Minister." Elliot jumped up on and yelled.

"Don't worry Pastor, I know Shereese, she is a level headed woman, I think if I had a serious talk about this, we can find out what the issue is and nip it in the bud." Minister Aaron said.

"No Minister, No means no."

"No means no? What are you talking about?"

Elliot calmed down and said, "I think that we should let God take care of this issue."

"You think so?"

"Yes, you know when God got ready to create the world, he could have done it in a moment, a twinkling of an eye."

"Yes."

"Well God took seven days. God took seven days because God was letting us know that even though you can do things quickly, sometimes you aughta just take your time and wait. Wait. Wait I say on the Lord." Elliot said in an impassioned plea.

"Well if you say so."

"I say so, and I beg of you, don't bring it up."

"OK, well, uh, the reason why I even said anything is that I know that there are some who are looking for a reason to get rid of you, so I think you ought to come on down to the church."

"I will be there minister."

Elliot walked over to the shower. He had set up his

whole day to be totally and completely free. He was going to watch a little television and nap for a good part of the day and then go out the evening and just enjoy the fact that he had money in his pocket (from the church gig) and a lot of time on his hands.

The thought of lying to Shereese about having ministry today didn't really bother him much. He figured that he was ministering to himself.

But all of that was gone now. He had to go to the church and put in some face time with the members.

He quickly showered and prepared. He put on his suit. He walked out to his car to get ready to drive over.

Elliot looked at his car which was still beat down. He made a mental note to go by the used car lot to buy a car fitting of his newfound stature as pastor of a church.

He went in the trunk and saw that he only had five quarts of oil. Elliot grabbed one quart and popped the hood and poured it in.

He jumped into the car and drove to the church. He was happy his car was able to reach 40 miles per hour today, it was a good day.

When he walked up to the church he saw Minister Aaron playing 2 on 2 basketball with a few teenagers at the park across the street.

The park looked like it once had been a nice one. There were a number of beat up and broken down swings. The big slide was in disrepair.

Elliot almost slipped in a pothole upon entering the

basketball court.

"Watch out Reverend. Don't fall down." One of the teenagers who was playing said. A short fat kid laughed at Elliot's misfortune.

"So preacher, do you play ball?" The laughing teenager asked.

"We got next." Elliot yelled.

Minister Aaron played pretty well, but his age did show and his team lost.

"How many old preachers do we have to beat today?" A tall lanky teenager who had just defeated Minister Aaron said.

"One more. If you can."

The kid laughed, "An old man and a fat runt."

The game started. Elliot passed often to his temporary teammate who was not very good. He was overjoyed to be playing, however.

The tall kid was playing Elliot closely, but Elliot was able to pass and shoot pretty effectively.

Minister Aaron cheered him on from the sidelines.

Eventually however, the inevitable happened and Elliot's team went down hard.

"Thanks for the game, but I gotta get to work."

"Next time you want a butt whipping, let me know." The teenager said.

Elliot snickered and walked out.

The short kid came over to Elliot and said, "Thanks, I can't remember when I had so much fun."

"What's your name?"

"Buster." The short kid said.

Then a car drove up and Shereese Harris yelled out the window, "Buster, it's time to go."

Buster ran towards the car. Shereese energetically yelled, "Hey Poppi."

"Shereese." Minister Aaron said.

"Pastor." Shereese said in a barely audible tone.

"Well hello, Sister Harris." Elliot said.

"You should have seen me, the pastor chose me." Buster said as he ran to the car.

"Buster there is Shereese's cousin. He started coming up every summer when we had a great youth program. But as you can see, the youth program is in great need of help."

"So those three kids and a broke down park are your youth program?" Elliot asked.

"No, Pastor Charles, those three kids and that broke down park is our youth program."

Elliot laughed.

"So what are we going to do about that?" Minister Aaron said.

"Good question." Elliot said. "But I will have a plan."

"I knew you would know. Let's get back to the church and get to work." Minister Aaron said as he led Elliot into the church across the street.

Chapter 14 - Elliot

As Minister Aaron and Elliot walked into the church building on the way to the office Elliot said, "OK, the first thing we can do is clean up that park. It is a shame that the park across the street from the church looks like that."

"Sounds good to me, if you can get them out there." Minister Aaron said.

Elliot frowned, "So are you saying that you have tried to get them out there?"

"I've tried, David tried, and the first lady tried. Everybody has tried, and nobody has been successful."

Minister Aaron stopped and then led the way to a door that had a nameplate on it, "Reverend Doctor Carl K. Charles." Above the name was the title, "Senior Pastor."

"We just had the nameplate done, I hope you like it."

Minister Aaron opened the door and led Elliot into it. He turned on the light and said, "No one has used it since Reverend Harris' demise. Make yourself at home."

Elliot looked at the big mahogany desk and chair and was pleased. He could not hide the smile that grew on his face.

"Ahh. So you are pleased." Minister Aaron said as he rushed out of the room.

Elliot walked back to the desk and sat own and yelled out the open door, "But back on that youth program. I am going to make this an initiative for my pastorate, you do know the children are the future." Elliot said.

Minister Aaron laughed as he walked back into the pastor's office. "Yes, didn't Whitney Houston tell us that?"

"I'm serious Minister." Elliot said.

"Well that park is the least of your worries. The real reason why I needed you to come in today is..." Minister Aaron pulled out a few letters that he had gone to retrieve.

"Here is a second warning for the light bill. It is five months overdue. They say that the lights will be cut off very soon." Minister Aaron said as he gave the letter to Elliot.

"Five months?"

"Here is the water bill, they have sent their bill into collections." Minister Aaron continued. He gave Elliot another letter.

"What? Why didn't you tell me this when I applied for the job?"

"Would you have accepted the job?"

Minister Aaron paused and then gave a final letter to Elliot. "And here is the church mortgage, we are a couple months behind."

Elliot smirked and asked, "Is that all?"

"Well no, we are behind on our dues to the convention, we can't vote in any elections. And we owe money to a few contractors. Deacon Miller fixed the toilets himself the last time they stopped up because we couldn't find a plumber that would work with us on credit."

"So what you are telling me is that I am the pastor of the Titanic and the fat lady is already singing our swan song?" Elliot said.

"What I am saying to you is that God put you here for such a time as this."

"I hate to ask this, but how does this affect my salary?"

"We got a few of the wealthy members of the congregation to pitch in to guarantee your salary for a couple of months. After that, your salary will have to come from the church treasury."

Elliot frowned, "Roughly speaking, what is the balance of the church treasury?"

"Well, it is on the upswing. Last time I looked it was 58 bucks." Minister Aaron said.

Elliot stood up and jumped. "58 dollars? How could that be, there were like 150 people in the audience last Sunday."

"It was 194 people, and not everybody pays who goes."

"I need to see the treasurer, this is ridiculous."

"Well you will, we have a staff meeting tomorrow. Today, you are going to go with me to the nursing home that the church supports."

"The church supports a nursing home ministry? The church doesn't even support its keep the lights on ministry."

"Well, as one of my pastors said, the gospel is free, but ministry costs."

Elliot thought, *Just like my salary.*

"We need to head over to the nursing home now, I am hoping to stop going all together and have you take over that responsibility." Minister Aaron said.

"OK, let's go."

Elliot was still reeling from what Minister Aaron had told him as they drove over to the nursing home.

"Pastor, I didn't want to pike it all on you, but you really needed to know. One preacher used to always say, 'Show me the worst of my case.' I figured I would do that."

"No, that was right, I have got to see what exactly is wrong before we can talk about what we are going to do to set it right." Elliot mustered up a smile as he looked at Minister Aaron.

"Now that is why God put you in this church at this time." Minister Aaron said.

"OK, so tell me about this nursing home, you said that the church supports it. How is it doing?"

"Financially? It is not doing much better than the church." Minister Aaron said as they continued to drive.

Elliot noted the area of town got worse as Minister Aaron had said.

"So, they are close to being kicked out of their building is what you are telling me?"

"Well, no, they have a few grants to keep it going, they wish they could take in more, but you know, we just can't afford expansion. You know the harvest is full but the laborers are few. But now we got one more laborer."

Minister Aaron slowly drove on a largely deserted urban street. A few kids were playing in the street. The buildings looked beat up and worn. Minister Aaron parked on the street in front of a building that looked like it had to be close to being condemned. It didn't look like a nursing home.

"Well, here we are."

Elliot laughed, "That is not a nursing home. In fact, it looks like an old condemned apartment complex."

"Well that is the Bethel Assisted Living Facility."

"Is that even wheelchair accessible?" Elliot asked.

"Well, we do pull out a ramp every once in a while, but when someone needs a wheelchair we have to find other housing options for them." Minister Aaron said.

"So you have a nursing home that can't take people with a wheelchair. You have a church that ain't paid its lights, water, or mortgage for at least the first quarter of this year, and you have a youth program that has no kids and no adequate play area. Is that everything?"

"You got it."

"So what am I supposed to do here today?"

"Well, it is your job to give a word of hope to the people. Just say something and then we will talk to the administrator."

"Minister Aaron, I need a word of hope for myself."

Minister Aaron laughed, "It will get better. It always gets better."

"I don't know how it could get worse." Elliot said as the two laughed. They walked towards the building.

Chapter 15 - Elliot

"We are a little late, we need to rush." Minister Aaron said to Elliot as they knocked on the front door of the building.

Elliot got a closer look at the building. The structure seemed to be a little more solid upon a closer look.

There was a pungent odor emanating from the door though. Minister Aaron picked up his arm to block his nose.

"It really smells in there, pastor. After a few minutes though you get used to it."

Elliot took a deep breath and said, "I've smelled worse."

Minister Aaron smiled as the front door opened.

A slender dark skinned woman in her mid-50s stood in front of them.

She shook Minister Aaron's hand. "Hello Minister, it is always good to see you," She said with a strong southern, but proper accent.

"Hello Kiona, You know our pastor Reverend Charles?"

"Pastor, yes, loved your sermon." She said as she shook Elliot's hand.

"Pastor this is Kiona Booth, the director of the facility." Minister Aaron said.

Elliot looked at her in her eyes, and she immediately diverted her eyes.

"Thank you Sister Booth." Elliot said.

"The people are waiting, please make your way to the back." Kiona said.

"Come on let's go." Minister Aaron said as he rushed him back. They walked down a hallway and to the left and right of them were doors, some open and some closed.

They rushed, but Elliot said "Hold on," as he stopped and looked in a room. In it was an elderly man who was sitting on a rocking chair.

"Hello, my name is Pastor Charles and I wanted to say hello." Elliot said, as he put out his hand to shake the old man's hand.

"I know who you are." The old man said quickly.

Elliot looked and saw what appeared to be a room of 100 square feet. There was a twin bed in there and a rocking chair and a dresser with a few books.

The smell of urine and sweat almost overpowered Elliot as he walked in to shake the man's hand.

"What do you want?" The man asked angrily.

"I just came to see about you and the other residents..." Elliot said.

"You came to stick your head in, preach a few words, whoop a little, and then go on back to your life." The man said.

"It ain't Sunday morning so I don't have to listen to you preach. I ain't got no money so I am sure you don't want to talk to me."

"Otis, show some respect." Minister Aaron said.

"I show respect to everyone who shows respect to me." Otis continued.

"No, hold on, Minister, let's hear the man out." Elliot said to Minister Aaron.

"Why are you angry with me?" Elliot asked.

"Why am I angry with you? You are the pastor of the church that is running this hell hole. Do you smell my room? Do you smell the hall? Do you see this place falling down?"

"Otis, leave the pastor alone." Kiona said.

"Speaking of people I don't respect, hello Kiona." Otis said.

Elliot thought about asking Kiona about the stench and disrepair that was all over the place, but thought better of it.

"We are late pastor." Minister Aaron said.

Elliot pulled out a piece of paper and wrote a number on it.

"This is my personal number, I want to talk to you about your experience so we can make things better."

"That is not necessary, I will tell you all you need to

know." Kiona said to Elliot.

"So are you telling me that I can't give one of my parishioners my phone number? Is that what you are saying?" Elliot said to Kiona.

"No, that isn't what she is saying, we just need to follow proper protocol." Minister Aaron said.

"We need to talk about this." Elliot said to both Kiona and Minister Aaron.

"Brother Otis, you call me." He said.

Kiona rolled her eyes and then Elliot said, "OK, let's get to the meeting."

Kiona led Minister Aaron and Elliot to the chapel.

"They have been waiting to hear you preach ever since you were announced as the new pastor." Kiona said.

Elliot whispered to Minister Aaron, "You didn't tell me that I was going to preach."

"I didn't? Forgive me, now here we are. We need a 30 minute sermonette."

Elliot frowned as he looked into the room. The door said chapel, but inside was a piano with discolored keys and 40 metal folding chairs with about three or four men and about two women, some half asleep, seated.

Elliot and Minister Aaron stood there as Kiona walked up to the front. "My brothers and sisters, I am happy to have with us today Pastor Charles from Bethel community church. Please welcome him."

Elliot looked at her and the people and then said, "It

stinks in here, why does it smell like we are in the sewer? Where is the bathroom?"

"That can wait pastor." Kiona said.

"These people can't think about anything but how bad it smells in here. Show me the bathroom."

That's right pastor." One man said.

"You ain't never lied." A younger woman said.

"It's right here." One of the residents took him to the bathroom. Elliot looked in there and saw that it wasn't in too bad of shape. It obviously looked like it had been cleaned today."

Elliot walked over to the toilet and flushed it. Immediately a strong odor came from the toilet.

"I know what the problem is."

"I'll call a plumber." Kiona said.

"No, where are your supplies?"

Kiona unlocked the door in the bathroom to the supply closet. Elliot walked in.

"Here it is." He pulled out a toilet wax ring and a wrench.

"I don't know about all the rest of this stuff, but I'm gonna fix this right now."

Minister Aaron said, "What about your suit."

"You are right, here take my jacket." He gave him his jacket.

He then reached back and turned off the water and grabbed a bucket to drain the water.

"You are not gonna work on the toilet in your suit."

Kiona said.

A group of residents congregated around.

"I ain't gonna preach when something is wrong that I can fix, I'll tell you that." Elliot said as he picked up the toilet and reached under and saw that the ring needed changing.

"Now this will go a lot faster if I had some help, if not, I'm willing to do it myself."

"I'll help." Otis said.

"No, if you get hurt we will…" Kiona said as Otis walked right by her to hold the toilet and help.

Elliot replaced the ring and they put the toilet back in place.

He reached behind the toilet and turned on the water which started filling up the toilet again.

"Some preachers don't like to get their hands dirty. I don't think I have ministered until my hands are dirty. Elliot said to the group of onlookers as he looked at Otis.

He then flushed the toilet.

The odor didn't come.

"Success. Now since you all are here, I'm gonna preach to you right here."

"You are not going to preach from the toilet?" Kiona said.

"It is a short sermon, changing the toilet was my introduction. Now Otis here said I have to preach."

Otis laughed.

So Elliot started preaching, "Today, is a new day, I

don't know who you had before, I don't know how things have gone before, but this day, I declare and decree that the enemy will not have this facility."

Some folks started shouting.

"I declare on this day, that this facility is gonna be like God would have it to be."

The residents started shouting as more came up.

"They say that the toilet is the throne. Well this is my throne right now. When you made me pastor, you made me king on this throne, and I declare that this is a new beginning."

People were shouting then.

"I want to ask you something today." Elliot said.

"How many people in here right now are willing to make this a better place?"

A few residents raised their hands.

"Staff, I'm talking to you too." He said as a couple of women wearing white walked up.

A couple raised their hands.

Elliot looked at Kiona who looked away again.

"Well my sisters and brothers, I will be here next week. And I expect a different attitude. I expect you to have your head up. I expect you to have a smile on your face in Jesus name."

The people started shouting.

"Now get out of here, I need some privacy."

Then everybody started laughing and exited the bathroom.

"That was amazing." Minister Aaron said.

"I'm serious, I got some stuff to do." Elliot said with a laugh.

Minister Aaron left as well.

Chapter 16 - Elliot

Elliot, Kiona Booth, and Minister Aaron sat in the small room. Elliot saw what appeared to be a kitchenette table with two old dining room chairs.

Kiona sat in the large chair behind the table. Minister Aaron sat on a metal folding chair on the other side of the table. Elliot sat next to Minister Aaron in a padded folding chair.

Four piles of neatly stacked papers were on the table. Behind Kiona was a bookshelf with many books stuffed into it.

"Sister Booth, in our last meeting you had some concerns." Minister Aaron said to Kiona, breaking the ice.

"Yes, we need more support from the church, we need more personnel, we need help with maintenance, we need..."

"Hold on, Now, I haven't looked much into it yet, but I doubt we can't do all of that right now." Elliot interrupted.

Kiona rolled her eyes and said, "Well, we are gonna

need a lot more than a preacher fixing a toilet."

Elliot laughed, "Well that is one less thing you can put on your list."

"I don't appreciate you disrespecting me in front of the residents. I work hard and you just got here trying to treat me like the maid." Kiona said.

"I spoke to one of my parishioners and you have a problem with that?" Elliot answered.

"I have a problem with preachers who don't know anything about anything rushing in here writing checks that the church ain't gonna cash."

"Well, from my understanding, financially you are well off."

"I don't know where you heard such a thing." Kiona said.

Elliot looked at Minister Aaron.

"Well, Sister Booth, what the pastor is trying to say is that even though we have financial issues here, this ministry is still in better financial shape than the rest of our ministries." Minister Aaron said.

"And from what I gather, that includes the health of the church as well, we are seconds away from getting our lights cut off." Elliot said.

"Well, that's your problem. My problem is getting these residents what they need."

"OK Sister Booth, tell me one thing you want me to do right now."

"We are going to get shut down if we don't have some

access ramps put on the front of this facility. Do that pastor." Kiona said with a slight sneer. "But I doubt it, my guess is that a new drum set for the church band or payment for a big time revivalist to come to town is more important."

"Now, we just told you that..." Minister Aaron said.

"I agree." Elliot said interrupting Minister Aaron.

"You agree? You agree with what?"

"I agree that we need access ramps in this building. And I agree that is more important than the music in the church. Let me get to work on this." Elliot said.

Kiona laughed, "Pastor, I'll believe that when I see it."

"Now what you are gonna do is get a handyman in here and take care of the easy jobs like I just did to the toilet. You get a handyman in here and I will get you the access ramps." Elliot said. He stood up and put out his hand to shake Kiona's.

"Deal?" Elliot said.

Minister Aaron looked shocked and interrupted, "I don't know if the church can afford..."

"Deal?" Elliot asked again, interrupting Minister Aaron.

"If you do this, I will vote myself for you to be the pastor." She stood up and shook his hand. She said, "Deal."

"By the way, what's the deal with Otis?" Elliot asked.

Kiona started looking through one of the stacks of papers on her desk and then said, "Here, right here is his file."

Elliot eyes widened and he refrained from yelling. He couldn't believe that the patient's records were sitting on a table.

"You can look at it if you wish, he has been a problem since his wife died and he lost touch with his son."

Elliot glanced at the papers and said, "Otis Carl. He is from New York state, how did he get here?"

"Traveling, car accident, his wife got it much worse, money ran out, and here he is." Kiona said.

"Well, thanks for meeting with me." Elliot said.

"I will see you in a few months." Kiona said.

"A few months? Why do you say next quarter? You will see me before then." Elliot said.

"Minister Aaron can only get over here once a quarter or so."

Elliot shook her hand and said, "I will see you next week."

She laughed as he and Minister Aaron walked out the door.

When they got outside the building Elliot couldn't hold it in any longer.

"This church is in shambles. Our youth program is nonexistent, our lights are about to get cut off, and our nursing home has an overworked and no doubt underpaid administrator who can't even afford a filing cabinet."

"You learned all that from this one conversation?"

"I know what I saw."

"I can't believe you promised her some ramps and that you were gonna be here next week."

Elliot smiled, "I have to report our progress."

"And what progress are you going to have in one week?"

Elliot continued to smile, "You will see."

"By the way, who owns these buildings? I see an old apartment complex over there." Elliot pointed. "And over there I see what appears to be an old drug store. Look over there, is that an old department store?"

"Well, when Reverend Harris first became pastor, he bought all of these buildings. That old department store was our first church building. We were going to turn that apartment complex into a low income housing facility. Phase one was to move the church out of that facility, which we did. Phase two was to open the nursing home. Phase three was to renovate that apartment complex. Phase three was to turn that department store into a bunch of small shops. Phase four..." Minister Aaron said.

"And none of that happened when the pastor died?" Elliot asked.

"When the pastor died, the church went into mourning. After that period of mourning, then we woke up with the reality of members leaving and no pastor wanting to come. But then God sent you here."

"So let me get this straight, the church owns all of

these buildings? And our church building is across town across from a broken down park?"

"Yes, it is all ours. By the way, that park used to be the best park in the city, but now, as you can see, it is like everything else, torn down and messed up."

They got back in their car and drove to the church. Elliot's mind was swirling with options and possibilities.

When they got back to the church and walked into the office, Elliot asked for the plans for the phases of Development.

Minister Aaron walked to the back closet and pulled out a tube that had in it a number of documents. "Here is the plan."

Elliot opened it up and saw the grand plan for the renewal of a city block.

Chapter 17 - Shereese

Shereese drove recklessly to the Grace Baptist City Temple where the community meeting was to be held.

She really did not know why she had to be there and was angry at both her boyfriend, Reverend David Michael, and her surrogate father, Minister Harold Aaron, for making her go to this meeting.

As she weaved in and out of traffic she spoke to her good friend Rachel Griffith, who was on the speaker phone.

"I don't know why you still fool with the church anyway, you have work to do and the church folks ain't even taking care of it." Rachel said.

"Well, I guess I am church folks. My father founded the church."

"You know what I mean." Rachel added.

"I don't really want to be here, but someone from the church had to come."

"Someone from the church, how about your man." Rachel said.

"Don't start nothing." Shereese said.

"Your man, oh yeah, he somewhere preaching ain't he? When is the last time you talked to him?"

"I talked to him last night."

"Yeah right…"

They set for a moment.

"Isn't the new pastor gonna go?"

"Well, Poppi said that I needed to go to the first meeting with Reverend Charles. Then he will go alone from here on out."

"Reverend Charles. Yeah that fine Reverend Charles, do you think I can get a counseling session with him?" Rachel joked.

"I will tell him he don't want no part of you." Shereese said quickly.

"Well, anyway girl, that is the kind of man you need to be with, not that fool you dating."

"Yeah, that's just what I need, someone to steal my cereal."

"I know you still ain't talking bout that cereal."

"You aren't gonna believe what he did."

"What? Who? The Reverend? Rachel asked.

"I get home last night and I get a delivery. I go to the door thinking it is some roses form David, turns out it is a box of Flavor O's."

"Ahh…Now that's sweet." Rachel interrupted.

"Yeah, well I don't trust him, and it is gonna take more than a box of cereal to win me over." Shereese said.

"Give the brother a chance, dang." Rachel said.

"I gotta go, I'm driving up to the church now."

Shereese hung up her cell phone and rushed out of the car.

The parking lot had about twenty cars in it. Shereese rushed into the building and over to the meeting.

She saw a number of preachers seated. She quickly saw an opening next to her pastor and eased over.

"Reverend Charles, sorry, I'm late." Shereese said.

"No need to worry sister, up till this point we have just had preachers trying to prove to each other they have done something." Elliot smiled.

Shereese looked at Elliot and gave a fake quick laugh.

"Sister Harris, might I ask what you had for breakfast this morning?" Elliot asked.

Shereese said, "And why might you ask that?"

Elliot smiled and looked back at Reverend A. C. Vannoy, the pastor of Grace Baptist City Temple where the meeting was being held.

Reverend Vannoy said from the front, "The main reason for this meeting is that we are going to start an initiative to win back our community. The initiative is called Operation Reach Back. I need some help in this program. We will directly attack the health problems and other issues in the community."

Someone raised their hand in the front.

Reverend Vannoy said, "Reverend Kelly, you have a question."

"Yes, what do you expect from us?"

"Reverend Vannoy answered, "Well, our multipurpose facility is being repaired now, so what I really need is a venue to kick off the program and a regular space to have health programs and other education programs."

It got quiet.

"Now certainly there are facilities that we can use for such a good program." Reverend Vannoy said.

Elliot raised his hand.

"What are you doing?" Shereese said to Elliot.

"The brother in the back, I don't think I know you." Reverend Vannoy said.

Elliot stood up, "My name is Reverend Carl K. Charles, the new pastor of Bethel Community Church, but folks call me Elliot."

Reverend Vannoy looked at him dismissively and said, "And how can I help you Reverend?"

"My church owns the buildings on a city block. With a little bit of work we can..." Elliot said.

"Ain't all those buildings condemned?" One preacher said.

"If they ain't they should be." Another said, which caused many to laugh.

"There is work to do, but none of those buildings are condemned." Elliot said.

"I don't know if we have the ability to get your facilities in working order." Reverend Vannoy said.

"Pastor, you have a building full of preachers who

have buildings but ain't letting you use them. I am a preacher with buildings and I will let you use them." Elliot said.

It got quiet and then one preacher said, "How dare you come in here and insult us. I for one have a lot of programs that I need my church for. Don't say what you don't know."

"I mean no disrespect. And if your church is being used, I am happy, but we all have buildings. Buildings we shout and praise in every weekend. But they lay empty during the week." Elliot said.

"What right do you have to tell us how to use our buildings?" Another preacher said angrily.

"I ain't telling nobody how to use any building, I'm just saying, I have some buildings if you want to use them." Elliot said.

Shereese looked at Elliot standing there and it reminded her of her father who often would fight some of these same pastors in these meetings in his attempts to minister to the community.

"Well, Reverend Charles makes a good point, if none of you are going to make your facilities available, then why shouldn't we use his facilities."

"A.C. this guy is trying to get us to fix up his broke down buildings. Don't fall for this." One elderly preacher said to Reverend Vannoy.

"How about this, my church will clean up the old department store that we used to worship in. And then you can use it." Elliot said.

Reverend Vannoy smiled and said, "I like this guy. So is there any other discussion?"

No one said anything.

"Operation Reach Back will happen at Reverend Charles facilities until our renovations are complete. Let us close out this meeting with prayer."

Elliot sat down. Shereese looked at him with admiration.

The meeting ended and Shereese asked Elliot, "So how are we going to clean up that old dusty building?"

"I will get the church to do it."

"Do you really think we can do this alone?"

"I read the plans, we will follow the plans."

"What plans?"

"Reverend Harris' plans to do real ministry, that's the plans I am going to follow."

"Reverend Charles?" A slim middle aged man said interrupting them.

"Yes."

"My name is Pastor Derek Cotter of the Seventh-day Proclaimers church, I know you are going to attempt to fix up your buildings."

"OK." Elliot said.

"I remember when Reverend Harris purchased those buildings. Back then he had a great vision. Anyway, I am going to talk to my deacons about helping you clean them up."

"Why Reverend Cotter, thanks."

"It's Pastor Cotter, we will support you every day but Saturday, the Sabbath."

"Pastor Cotter, your help will on any day will be appreciated."

"Here is my number." Pastor Cotter gave Elliot a card. "Please call me with the specifics.

"Looks like God is already providing help in the time of need." Elliot said to Shereese.

Shereese wanted to smile but said, "I think we need to get the church on board before you start celebrating."

Elliot said in his preacher's voice, "Don't wait till the battles over, shout now..."

Shereese walked out of the church. Elliot stayed back to talk to some of the other ministers who were making their way over to him.

Chapter 18 - Shereese

At church the next Sunday morning around 350 members were in attendance. Attendance had held steady since Elliot became pastor. Shereese figured it was due to people attempting to feel out the new administration.

Shereese found her regular seat next to her mother Lady Harris. She filed in and sat next to her.

The choir was in the middle of a hymn that the director had turned into an upbeat gospel song.

"Where's David?" Lady Harris asked Shereese.

Shereese looked up at the front of the church and saw that David's seat was empty.

"I don't know, maybe he got called to preach somewhere?" Shereese answered.

"You don't know? Do you talk to him?"

"Yes, but…" Shereese began to answer.

She remembered the difficulties she had been having recently as David had become more distant. She wondered if their relationship was going forward or not. And on a deeper level, she wondered if she even wanted to be in a relationship with him.

"Shhh. We're in church." Shereese said to her mother as she turned to see the choir continue to sing.

"Don't shush me." Lady Harris frowned and then a smile entered her face as she turned to look at the service.

Shereese couldn't help but find her eyes slowly gravitating to Elliot. He had a dignified smile on his face.

She tried to summon up to mind her original anger at him, but it was almost all totally dissipated.

Seeing him work with the church and even deal with other ministers, and finally, seeking to push her father's plan into action, had really made her admiration for him to grow.

Elliot stood up to take the pulpit during an announcements phase of the service.

"My sisters and brothers, I have only been the pastor for a few weeks, but I am seeing a lot of challenges that we face."

"Yes Lord." Someone said in the congregation.

"And I don't mean to step on no toes, but we need help, and if I don't step on toes, I don't know if your feet will get to steppin." Elliot said with a smile.

A few in the congregation laughed.

"Now, Sister Shereese Harris and I have met with some preachers in the city. At this meeting Reverend A. C. Vannoy from Grace Baptist has suggested that we have an Operation Reach Back. Here we are reaching to help the community's physical, spiritual, and emotional needs."

"All right now." A woman in the congregation said.

"Then Reverend Vannoy asked for a venue, and no one raised their hand." Elliot continued.

"I then remembered that Bethel has a building."

It kind of got quiet in the church.

"I said, Bethel not only has an auditorium, but Bethel has a few buildings."

It was still quiet, but Elliot continued.

"But these buildings need some work. Now Pastor Cotter from the Proclaimers church has offered to help us, but I want to make an appeal now for members to come help us clean up this auditorium."

It then got very quiet. A baby started crying in the corner of the church, but that was the only noise in the church.

"So right now, if you are willing to help clean up OUR building, then I ask you to stand right now."

No one stood.

"Is there anyone?" Elliot said.

Then eighty-five year old Mother Jenkins stood up.

"OK, I have one, is there any others?"

Then Otis Carl from the nursing facility stood up. Elliot smiled.

Shereese and Lady Harris stood up.

Then Minister Aaron stood up.

But then no one else stood.

Elliot's countenance fell as he fell into his seat.

Shereese felt like jumping up to encourage him as it really seemed to be a blow to him.

The next part of the service began as Minister Aaron prayed and then there was another choir song.

A smile grew on Elliot's face and then he stood up and walked down from the pulpit and walked down the aisle while the song was going on. He then walked out the back of the church.

About thirty minutes later, it was time for the sermon and the pulpit was empty. A few people were talking when Minister Aaron walked up to the pulpit and said, "Let's sing a hymn to prepare our hearts for the message."

"No need, I'm ready." Elliot yelled from the back of the church.

He had changed from his suit to his jeans and looked to be in work clothes. He walked up to the pulpit.

"I was going to preach about standing firm in your blessing."

"Go head." Someone said.

"But, I just didn't feel like preaching that." Elliot continued.

It got quiet.

"I want your church folks to stop talking about getting your blessing and start being a blessing." Elliot said.

"I was sitting here thinking that the greatest sermon, I could do today is to go working on cleaning up that building so that it can be a blessing for somebody else."

Yes." Mother Jenkins said.

"So what was I doing in the back room? I was calling Pastor Cotter, and I told him that I and my church is gonna be working on cleaning that building today, so if bring his people over on this Sunday Morning."

"All right now."

"I got on my jeans and I am ready to work. I don't care if it is one of you, two of you, or 400 of you, we are going to work." Elliot said.

"Yes sir. Otis shouted.

"Go home, put on your working clothes. Because like some preachers I ain't saying 'go ye.' I am saying 'go we.'"

Elliot then said, "I ain't gonna say the benediction, because our cleaning up that building is our sermon. Our working for the community is our worship. I'll see you at the building in a couple hours. When we finish, then we will have the benediction." He smiled and started walking out the back of the church.

Mother Harris looked at Shereese and said, "He reminds me of your father, he is going to get things done."

Shereese smiled and said, "It sure looks that way."

A few of the members were angry. Shereese heard people complaining about no real sermon. Then there were others defending Elliot's choice.

Minister Aaron then walked up to the microphone and said, "The pastor has called us out to work, if you can, then we expect to see you out there, I'm going home to put on my clothes right now, we'll see you out at the building."

Chapter 19 - Elliot

Elliot drove up to the old building and saw about six cars and a church van from the Seventh Day Proclaimers church.

He parked his car and examined the outside of the building. This time he looked a bit closer than he had before when he and Minister Aaron had initially seen it.

Before, he was looking at its possibilities. But now, he was looking at its realities and it shocked him.

There were four steps at the entrance of the building. And two of them were broken. It appeared someone had stacked some concrete blocks there to allow entrance.

At the entrance it appeared that at any time something would fall and hurt anyone who happened to be there.

Elliot looked up and saw that all six windows were broken. He shook his head as years of disrepair were evident.

Someone honked the horn. Elliot saw it was Minister Aaron who was parking out front.

Elliot walked into the building and almost tripped.

He looked down and saw that even the concrete bricks that they were using were starting to fall apart.

He walked in and saw Pastor Cotter and about four other men all dressed in work clothes. He saw the feisty 80 year old Mother Jenkins and Otis and Shereese and Lady Harris.

Minister Aaron walked into the building.

Elliot walked over to Shereese ad Lady Harris who were standing there watching.

Mother Jenkins had found one of those large sweepers and was sweeping and Otis was cleaning up some glass.

"So how is it going?" Elliot asked.

Lady Harris laughed, "It is going bad, but every great journey begins with one step."

Elliot smiled.

"Rev Charles." Pastor Cotter said to Elliot when he saw him.

Elliot was really getting tired of everyone calling him Reverend Charles. He wondered how long he would be able to continue the charade and sometimes he thought he would just tell them, but not now.

"Yes, pastor." Elliot said as he walked over and shook his hand.

"This man here is a member of my church, Trever Jones. He owns an electrician business."

"Brother Jones, I am so happy you were able to get here."

"Well Reverend, I am not sure if you are gonna like what I have to tell you. I got good news or bad news, depends on how you take it."

"Well someone said once to show me the worst of my case, so go on with it." Elliot answered.

"It is gonna take in the neighborhood of thirty thousand dollars to fix this building electrically. Now I ain't a builder, but from what I can see, she looks worse than she actually is. A little cosmetics and you will be on the road." Brother Jones said.

"Brother Jones, so what? You saying we are forty to fifty thousand dollars away from using this facility?"

"Probably a little less than that. But then you will be in business."

"Well the church ain't got that kind of money. You might as well have told me a million dollars." Elliot said.

"Well, for a building this size that hasn't been used for as long as this one you are lucky that it is so low."

Mother Jenkins was still working.

"So what do you want to do?" Minister Aaron asked.

The door opened and four other members walked in the door.

Elliot thought about it. He knew that there was no money. "I am not sure."

"When we started this church we never had the money to do anything we needed to do before the time." Lady Harris said.

"I know that's right." Mother Jenkins said as she

stopped sweeping for a moment.

"Brother Otis, remember when the heater went out that Christmas?" Lady Harris asked.

He laughed, "How could I forget, your husband went to the repair shop with fifty dollars in his pocket and came back with a thousand dollars and the heater fixed."

Lady Harris laughed.

"It's not about what you got, it's about who got you and young man, God got you, I can tell it. I heard it in you." Lady Harris said to Elliot.

"I saw it too, what are we gonna do? We are gonna fix this place up and use it for the glory of God." Minister Aaron said.

Elliot felt a smile emerging on his face and said, "OK, Brother Jones, you do whatever you can do, we will take care of."

Brother Jones looked at Pastor Cotter who shook his head in the affirmative.

"OK, I need to go get my tools, so we can get to work." Brother Jones said.

"Mother Jenkins, where did you get that broom?"

"Round back."

"Show us where you got it and you take a break." Elliot said.

"I ain't tired yet." Mother Jenkins said.

"Now Mother Jenkins we don't want you hyperventilating out here."

"If you want me to stop then you best stop your

yapping and get out here and help me finish."

Elliot laughed, "OK, let's get out here and help her. Let's clean up all we can clean up." Elliot said.

Elliot joined the group who was sweeping, but from time to time he couldn't help as his eyes would catch Shereese who was also sweeping.

"You know pastor, she may be dating someone, but she ain't married." Minister Aaron said to him.

"Now what are you talking about."

"I see where you looking." He shook his head as he swept on by Elliot.

A lot of thoughts swirled in Elliot's head as he swept. The burden of the church's responsibilities came on him. The reality that he was not who he has said he was also weighed on him.

But at the same time the lovely Shereese Harris seemed to brighten his mind. He replayed her smile in his head whenever he was not catching a glance of her from time to time as they worked.

A few hours passed and the sun began to set in the distance.

David Michael then walked in the building. "I couldn't believe them when they told me. Y'all are actually fixing this place up!" David yelled.

"Reverend Michael, you here to help?" Elliot asked.

"Well, no, But I came to send my regards, I have to go preach."

"Why are you always preaching whenever it is time

to do some real work?" Otis asked.

"God called me to preach, he called you to sweep." David responded.

"Well he called me to preach and sweep." Elliot said.

David ignored him and walked over to Shereese. It appeared they were having an argument. David seemed to be asking her to leave, but she wasn't ready to leave.

"Well folks, it is getting a bit late, and I don't think we should be walking around in this after dark, so I thank you all, and I will be in touch."

They began to leave.

"Hold up pastor, you never gave the benediction." Otis asked.

"Huh?"

"You said we would be having worship in this building, now you need to give the benediction."

Elliot laughed and asked them all to hold hands as they closed out. When they all met in a circle David started praying.

"Our dear merciful Father, we thank you so much being the light that we needed."

"Yes Lord." Mother Jenkins said as everyone else stood quiet.

"We thank you for being mercy to those who need mercy. We thank you for being hope for those who need hope." David continued.

Elliot looked and saw Minister Aaron shaking his head and David continued praying for a few more minutes.

"And now we ask you to be with us as we leave. Bless us and strengthen us in the almighty name of Jesus Christ, amen."

A few of the members shook their heads as they left the building. Pastor Cotter and Brother Jones came over to Elliot who stared as David and Shereese walked out together.

"Pastor Charles?" Pastor Cotter asked.

"Yes, Yes..." Elliot said as the voice shook him out of his stupor.

"We are ready whenever you need us." Pastor Cotter said.

"I did all I can do for free, but the rest is gonna cost. I will send you a list of what needs to be done so that you won't get taken by any unscrupulous contractors." Brother Jones said.

"Well, I don't know who better to do this job than the one who has already done so much for free, give me the bill and I will see what I can do about paying it. Thanks man." Elliot said as he shook his hand.

Chapter 20 - Shereese

The first Monday evening of every month was a Trustees meeting. Shereese walked into the church. There were more attendees than usual.

She opened the sanctuary and saw what looked like thirty people yelling at each other while Minister Aaron tried to calm them down. He stood at the podium in front of the people yelling.

"Order, sisters and brothers, please calm down, we must have order." Minister Aaron said.

"Can you believe this guy, making all these changes without going through proper channels?" Shereese heard one member say to her left.

Shereese saw her mother and walked over to her.

"Why are they so angry?" Shereese asked her mother.

"Well some of these people think the pastor is making changes too quickly." Lady Harris said.

Shereese looked behind her and saw one of her friends with a sour look on her face.

"Denise, what's the matter?" Shereese asked.

"This new pastor is changing things. Just like

Reverend Michael said…"

"Hold up. What did David say?" Shereese said.

"He said that Reverend Charles is trying to eliminate the board of trustees."

"I don't know anything about that." Shereese said.

Denise looked confused, "You need to talk to him. He is in the pastor's study with a few members right now."

Shereese walked to the back room and saw a relatively calm meeting going on. Deacon Miller, Reverend Michael, and the treasurer, Tanya Ward, were there. David had just gotten finished saying something when it all went quiet.

"What is going on?" Shereese said.

"This man is not worthy of your daddy's church." Deacon Miller said.

"So you are meeting behind closed doors making up lies about him?"

"What lies?" Deacon Miller asked.

"Someone told me that he is going to dismantle the board of trustees."

"That is not a lie. I didn't believe it myself until both the treasurer and Reverend Michael confirmed it." Deacon Miller said.

"And how do you two know this?" Shereese asked.

"We don't have time for this. We need to set him down before he chairs his first meeting of the trustees." Reverend Michael said.

Shereese heard the noise quiet immediately. And then

they heard Minister Aaron say, "Let us now hear the pastor that according to the bylaws should chair this meeting."

Reverend Michael stood up and said, "If we are going to do this, we must do it now, let's go do this." Reverend Michael and Tanya walked out first. Deacon Miller looked at Shereese and shrugged his shoulders and walked out. Shereese followed them.

Elliot was on the way to walking up to the microphone when Reverend Michael asked for the microphone to which Minister Aaron gave it to him.

"My sisters and brothers, it appears that we have made a big mistake in hiring Reverend Charles as the pastor of this church. Deacon Miller, Sister Tanya Ward, and Sister Shereese Harris all stand with me requesting that the church rescinds its invitation to Reverend Harris to pastor this church."

There was a pause. *I don't stand in support of that!* Shereese thought as she immediately looked at Elliot. Elliot's face looked flush before changing to resolve.

"So in line with that, I move that we rescind that invitation."

"On what basis?" Minister Aaron asked.

"There is a motion on the floor, call for the vote." Reverend Michael said.

"Your motion is out of order." Minister Aaron responded.

Then a big groan came from the auditorium.

At that point Elliot reached the front of the church. Elliot looked at Reverend Michael. "Reverend Michael." Elliot said.

"Reverend Charles." David shook his head and said.

Elliot looked at Deacon Miller, Tanya, and Shereese

"So what's going on?" Elliot asked Minister Aaron.

"It appears a group of people want to remove you as pastor."

"OK. I want to call this meeting into order." Elliot said into the microphone.

"There is a motion on the floor." Reverend Michael yelled.

"I told you, your motion was out of order." Minister Aaron said.

Elliot smiled, and said, "OK, take the vote."

"What?" Minster Aaron answered.

"Take the vote."

Minister Aaron said weakly, "OK, there is a motion on the floor to rescind the invitation to make Reverend Charles the pastor. Is there a second."

"Deacon Miller said, "Second..."

"OK, it is time for the question." Minister Aaron said.

"I have a question. Upon what basis do you seek to remove me?"

"We don't need a reason. Our reason is we made a mistake putting you in." Reverend Michael said.

"Certainly there is a reason." Elliot said. He walked in to the audience with a microphone. "You look like you want me removed."

"You got that right." The elderly woman said.

"OK, why?"

"Well you want to remove the trustees of power, and I am not ok with that." The elderly woman continued.

"I do not want to do that, I will not do that. In fact, I do not even have the authority to do that. Isn't that right Reverend Michael?" Elliot asked.

Nobody said anything.

"I'm asking you a question Reverend Michael, can the pastor eliminate the board of trustees?"

"No…" Reverend Michael said.

"Elliot smiled, OK, what else you got?"

"You are spending money that we just don't have." Someone yelled.

"Now I think that Sister Ward can field this one, I'm glad you are standing up there so accessible and ready to answer. How much money have I spent as pastor of this church?" Elliot asked Tanya.

"You have spent no money yet, but your plans would cost a lot of money." Tanya answered.

"OK, let's deal with this right now. All my plans have spent is a few brooms for Mother Jenkins to sweep up an old building."

"Now come on Reverend Charles, to fix up that building it is gonna cost 30K. That is 30 thousand dollars we don't have." Reverend Michael said smugly.

Elliot pulled out a piece of paper and said. "OK,

Shereese and Tanya, I'm looking at the church budget. We can't afford to fix up a building to do ministry, but we can afford to pay five thousand dollars a week for a television show that Reverend Michael hosts. Is that true?"

Shereese smiled. Tanya looked at Reverend Michael sadly and said, "Yes."

"So you are spending a quarter of a million dollars on a TV show to promote one man, but you can't afford 30K for real ministry?"

"Now hold on, that television show is ministry." Reverend Michael said

"Deacon Miller, how many people have joined the church from that so called ministry?" Elliot asked.

Deacon Miller said, "One maybe two a year."

"How many people could we have fed for a quarter of a million dollars in a year? How many people could we teach to read with a quarter of a million dollars?"

"That is all beside the point, that ministry was put into effect by the trustees." Reverend Michael said.

"OK, let's look at the music in this church, that's some great music, but how much does that cost a week?"

Tanya said, "250 bucks per person for the band, altogether 1 thousand bucks a week."

"So that's 50 Thousand a year. You are paying 50 thousand a year to entertain the saints but you can't spend 30 thousand to do real ministry." Elliot said.

Lady Harris was smiling from ear to ear, as was

Minister Aaron.

"I don't see you working for free. Ministry costs money." Reverend Michael said.

"Speaking of which, why do you make more money than the interim pastor and you ain't even here most of the time." Elliot said.

"You are not going to attack me personally." Reverend Michael said.

"You got the money, but it ain't gonna cost you a thing to fix that building." Elliot said.

"How can you say that? The man said thirty thousand dollars." Reverend Michael said.

"I trust God is gonna pay for it. And if God don't pay for it, then take it out of my salary." Elliot said.

There was a big uproar at that point.

"There is a motion on the floor. There is a motion on the floor." Reverend Michael was yelling trying to get everyone to calm down.

"Is there any more discussion?" Minister Aaron asked. Nobody said anything.

"All in favor of the motion to rescind our invitation to pastor Charles to be pastor of the church say aye."

There was a small number of people shouting in affirmation.

"All opposed say nay."

And an obvious greater number said nay.

"The motion is defeated." Minister Aaron said.

"I want a hand count." Reverend Michael said.

"OK, all of those who are in favor of the motion to rescind the pastor's invitation show it by raising your hand."

Reverend Michael, Tanya Ward and a few others raised their hand.

"All opposed, please raise your hand."

Shereese, Lady Harris, Deacon Miller, and most of the rest of those in attendance raised their hands.

"Y'all are gonna be sorry." Reverend Michael said. He walked out of the church.

Elliot walked up to the front and said, "Now that all of that madness is out of the way, let's get down to business."

Chapter 21 - Shereese

Shereese turned to walk down to her seat. Elliot said, "Hold on, I'm gonna need to talk to you, Minister Aaron, Deacon Miller, and Sister Ward."

Elliot then turned to the people and said. "Now my sisters and brothers. You need to know that financially we are strapped. Our lights are getting ready to get cut off."

"What?" Someone yelled. A mild roar arose from the people.

"Hold on, hold on." Elliot said. "Now, I am going to work with the ministerial committee to come up with some real cuts to set us on a sound financial footing."

The crowd began to change.

A middle aged woman in the middle of the congregation raised her hand.

"Yes..." Elliot said.

"No one told us about any financial issues until now."

Elliot looked at Minister Aaron who shrugged his shoulders.

"Well guess what, I'm gonna tell you all everything.

It is time for everything to come out. Just give me two weeks. In two weeks I will come up with a plan to straighten this church up financially." Elliot said.

A well-dressed man in his mid-twenties raised his hand.

Elliot pointed to him and asked, "What is your question?"

"So you are promising to fix all of the issues in two weeks and you expect us to believe that?"

"No, I am promising to give you a plan that if followed will set us on sound footing. All I want from you is the power to deal with the salaries in this church. We are spending too much." Elliot said before a lot of noise came up from the audience.

A man in overhauls raised his hand.

"OK, what is your question?" Elliot asked.

"I'm the handyman. I have always been the handyman. And I am paid by the church. How can I trust that you will be fair? The board of trustees voted me in so the board of trustees needs to fire me if need be." The man said.

"I work for the church too." Someone else said. "And what about my keys?" Another individual said.

Shereese was shocked at the number of people who seem to now be on the payroll. Shereese walked up to the microphone and asked, "How many receive income from the church."

Tanya walked up to the microphone and put her hand

over it and said to Shereese, "That is not a good question. There are many different reasons that people are receiving money. Answering that question could…"

Elliot interrupted her and asked her to take her hand off the microphone.

Elliot said, "See this is the problem, we are spending money everywhere, nobody knows where or how much. Now I understand you are afraid of losing your income, but we do understand we have to fix this."

"Fix what? Are you gonna fix the toilet when it overflows?" The man in overhauls said. A few people laughed.

"If I have to." Elliot said.

"So you are trying to take my job." The man said and it got loud again.

"OK, I want a vote enabling me to change the payments for worship ministers. I will bring the rest of my plan to the church two weeks from now."

"Do I hear a motion to enable the pastor to change the financial structure of the worship ministries?"

Tanya whispered to Shereese, "David is gonna be mad."

"So Move." Someone in the audience said.

"Is there a second?" Elliot asked.

"I second." Minister Aaron said.

"Is there any discussion?"

The man with overhauls said, "So you are not gonna touch maintenance."

"No…"

"Just worship?" Someone else asked.

"Exactly." Elliot said.

"Any more questions?" Elliot asked.

It was quiet.

"All in favor say Aye."

The response was kind of lackluster.

"All opposed say nay."

It also was lackluster, but the motion obviously passed.

"OK, I want to talk to the ministerial committee now. I will leave Minister Aaron over this meeting. Minister Aaron please come after you close out this meeting."

Elliot, Tanya, Deacon Miller, and Shereese walked into the back room.

When they fully got into the room, Elliot slammed the door and said, "OK, I need to know what is going on?"

He walked over to Deacon Miller and asked him, "What was that about? So you want me out?"

"Well, at first, I mean Reverend Michael said that you were making some changes." Deacon Miller said.

"And it is obvious he was right." Tanya said.

Elliot smiled. And you. He looked at Shereese.

"I didn't know anything about this meeting."

"OK, well, it looks like I am in hostile territory and y'all can't even tell me the truth." Elliot's eyes flared.

"The few financial records I could get out of Tanya are really messed up. I ain't an accountant, but it appears as though you have been spending more than you have been taking in for years."

"That couldn't be true." Shereese said.

"Let me finish before you interrupt me Sister Harris." Elliot said angrily.

Shereese was a bit taken about by his tone and wanted desperately to tell him she was not involved with the attempted coup, but sat their quietly.

Minister Aaron walked in.

"Minister Aaron, what side are you on?" Elliot asked.

"What...what do you mean?" Minister Aaron replied.

"He thinks everybody is out to get him, he wants to know if you were involved." Shereese said.

"No, No. I am with you."

"We'll see." Elliot said shortly.

"The musicians are making 1 thousand dollars a week. That is going to be 250 dollars a week starting this Sunday." Elliot said.

"You just cut their money from 250 dollars apiece to 50 dollars? Who is gonna tell them?" Minister Aaron said.

"I don't care who tells them." Elliot said still in an angry tone.

"Calm down pastor." Minister Aaron said.

Elliot looked at him with a hard stare.

"Reverend Michael's salary is eliminated." He looked at Shereese as he said it. Shereese looked away.

"What?" Tanya said.

"I've been here eight weeks and he is never here. His salary is eliminated as of right now. Do you have anything to say Sister Harris?"

Shereese was getting irritated at Elliot's tone and said, "What do you want me to say?"

"All the other ministers' salaries will be cut by 25%. You got anything to say Minister Aaron?"

"I think you need to calm down and think about this." Minister Aaron said.

Elliot ignored him. "And finally, that television program is gone. Totally and completely." Elliot said as he looked at every member sitting in that room.

"Who gets to tell him the good news?" Elliot said. "I bet he'll find out soon enough."

Elliot then looked at Tanya. "I would fire you but the church didn't give me the power to fire the treasurer."

"Reverend Charles. This ain't you." Minister Aaron attempted to get him to stop talking.

Elliot continued "...Your treasurer skills are so bad I don't know if it is due to incompetence or malice, but I'm gonna find out soon enough."

A tear began to come in Tanya's eye.

"Would you shut up Pastor?" Minister Aaron said.

"I ain't done. And you Sister Harris." Elliot looked at Shereese.

Shereese put her hand on her hip and looked at Elliot square in his eyes.

Minister Aaron then said, "OK, that's it. No more.

Everybody out of the room. I need to talk to the pastor."
Minister Aaron said.

"I ain't done yet." Elliot said.

"I've heard enough, everybody out, ain't nothing happened yet, I'll see you at the next meeting. Please keep this all under wraps." Minister Aaron said.

Elliot looked at Minister Aaron and said, "Fine…" He then stared back at Shereese.

The rest of the group filed out the room leaving Elliot and Minister Aaron. Shereese heard yelling on the other side of the door as she left.

Chapter 22 - Elliot

"These church folks are getting on my last nerve Jeremy." Elliot said to his roommate."

"You mean the church folks you lied to make them hire you as their pastor?" Jeremy said.

"Naw, I didn't lie to them till after they offered me the job." Elliot said before snickering at how crazy that statement was.

"See, you don't even believe that yourself." Jeremy said as they both laughed.

"Come on man, I'm serious. This church is turning around cause of my work and every step of the way they trying to get rid of me."

"El, I have to admit that this church is a good look for you. You ain't as trifling as you usually are."

"I guess that is a compliment." Elliot interrupted.

"BUT...You are still not being totally upfront with them. God is blessing no doubt, but there is a limit to that blessing as long as you base this ministry on a lie."

"So what do you suggest?"

"I suggest that you tell them there was a mistake and

be done with it."

"And then they will fire me and it will be all over."

"Well, you asked me my suggestion." Jeremy said.

There was a moment of silence.

"OK, what is your plan?" Jeremy asked breaking the silence.

Elliot smiled, "I wondered when you were gonna ask me that. I am going to implement Reverend Harris' plan and totally turn this church around. Then I will tell them who I am and it won't matter. They will elect me as the pastor and then we will be on the road to success."

Jeremy laughed. "Your plan has failure written all over it."

"Well, that is the plan."

"OK, and what do you need for me to do?"

"Well, since you a lawyer, I wanted you to help me find a way to get the front entrances of my buildings fixed. Our nursing home needs some ramps and our entrance into our old facility needs to be fixed. It is gonna cost 30K just to fix the…"

"Did you say ramps for a nursing home?"

"Yeah man, how come?"

"Well, last year our practice was involved in a multimillion dollar lawsuit against the city because they didn't provide adequate ramping off the city streets into buildings."

"OK, so what?"

"Well the city settled and set aside a chunk of money

to provide ramps off the city streets."

"How do I get them to work on my street?"

"You have a nursing home. That nursing home doesn't have adequate ramping?" Jeremy asked.

"That's what I said?"

"And how long has this been the case?"

"I would say, years, but don't know for sure."

Jeremy smiled. "The city should have been calling you and not you calling the city."

"Well, I don't think anybody has called us."

"I am sure my boss wants to hear this. Can you and your people come to a meeting with the city in a couple days? We have been waiting for something like this to come along." Jeremy smiled.

"So does this mean you don't want me to tell them who I am?" Elliot asked.

"Not just yet..." Jeremy smiled.

***

"What do you want?" Shereese said in the phone to answer Elliot's call.

She was still angry at how Elliot had treated her during the last meeting.

"And why are you angry? I should be mad at you, the way you and your cronies..."

"They were not my cronies."

"Well, I show up to my first meeting of the trustees

132

and you and your boyfriend staged a coup."

Shereese felt like continuing the fight, but she quickly realized that nothing good was coming from the discussion right now.

"I repeat, Reverend Charles, what do you want?"

The phone went dead for a moment when Elliot said, "I have a meeting with the mayor tomorrow. I and an attorney. We are going to talk about the need to add access ramps to our facilities that we are rejuvenating."

Shereese was still mad, but she still couldn't help but smile about the fact that her father's plan was going forward and somebody actually cared about it.

"What is this about?"

"Well, the city should have given us this access before now. Our lawyers think that we might be able to parlay their inaction into them doing more than they might otherwise have done."

Shereese couldn't help but be excited at this point.

"But, how do you have a lawyer, we don't have a lawyer, how are you paying the lawyer?" Shereese said.

"God has provided." Elliot said.

"And how has God provided, we don't have any money."

"Your pastor has friends in high places." Elliot said. "Maybe you should think about that the next time you try to vote him out."

"Reverend Charles, I didn't want to vote you out, I never did."

"So now you are gonna tell me that you and your man are my most loyal supporters?"

"No. David wants you out. He is working to set you down, but I am not in that."

"Hmmm." Elliot said.

"And Pastor Charles, you seem to keep referring to David as my man, does it bother you that I am dating him?"

There was an awkward silence.

"No, I just wanted…"

"Why are you so mad at me?"

"You attacked me Shereese."

"No, I was standing there, and you never gave me a chance to explain. Why didn't you let me explain?"

"So now you are gonna tell me that you and your man weren't trying to attack my ministry."

"There you go, calling him my man again. When are you going to admit why you are so angry?"

"Admit what?" Elliot said.

"You know what I'm talking about." Shereese elevated her voice.

Shereese sat in anticipation wondering if he would say something.

"Well, I don't know about that, but I do know that we need to go put your daddy's plan in action." Elliot said changing the subject.

"I appreciate you Elliot, ah, Reverend Charles."

Shereese said surprising even herself.

"I would never attack your ministry. I have seen it in action. I know you are the real deal." Shereese continued.

"I appreciate that, and I probably shouldn't have jumped to the conclusion, but your man...ah, I mean Reverend Michael is making it more difficult to minister effectively in the church."

Shereese thought for a moment and said, "I wish I had met someone like you a few years ago."

"Why?"

The door opened and David walked into the room.

"I uh, I need to go." Shereese said into the phone and then she turned to David, "Hi, David."

"Hey baby." David said.

"I have Pastor Charles on the line, he may have found a way to pay for the access ramp improvements." Shereese said.

David sneered and took the phone.

"Reverend Charles. We ain't got time for this now. We will get back to you later." The then clicked the phone.

"David, why you gonna be like that?" Shereese asked David.

David looked at Shereese and stopped. He then looked closer. "There ain't nothing going on is there?"

"What, why?"

"I just want to know..."

"What are you accusing me of?"

"You like this fool don't you?"

"Show some respect."

"You know what, I've been looking into Reverend Charles, and I just got the feeling that something ain't right bout him."

"What do you care? We are leaving this church right?"

"Well…"

"What do you mean well?"

"I've been trying to tell you for a little while, it seems that the church in LA has fallen through."

"Fallen through? And how long have you known this?"

David angrily looked at her, "Why are you acting all crazy, I thought you didn't want to leave your city. So now, guess what, we get to stay in Atlanta, and I get to take over your father's church."

"We already have a pastor."

"They have an interim pastor, but I will let them know that I want to become a candidate for the church, then we can get rid of this preacher and start our life together?"

"So is that a proposal?"

"A proposal? I mean, huh?" David was taken aback.

"I just wonder if I'm even in your life, you make all the decisions without my input."

Shereese was getting more and more angry.

"So this is why you are trying to get Reverend Charles out of the church. You want to be the pastor now."

"The people love me, your mom loves me, and you love me. There is no room for Pastor Charles."

"So when are you gonna tell Minister Aaron?"

"I know you love him, but he don't like me, I am going to tell the next meeting of the ministerial advisory."

"Well, I'm gonna tell him."

"Shereese, come on now."

"And I'm gonna tell Reverend Charles."

"What! Whose side are you on?"

"I'm on my daddy's side now please leave. I have some work to do, I can't even look at you right now."

"Come on Shereese…"

"Get out." Shereese yelled.

David slowly walked out of Shereese's apartment.

Chapter 23 - Elliot

"This is Reverend Charles of Bethel Community Church." Jeremy said to the Mayor, a pudgy black man with gray speckled in his hair.

The mayor smiled and stood up from behind his desk and reached out to shake Elliot's hand.

"Oh yes, I am hearing good things about what you are doing in the community." The mayor said.

"And it is good to see you again." The mayor said to Shereese.

Elliot laughed inwardly. *This guy is full of it*. He thought to himself as he took his seat.

Elliot looked over at Jeremy who immediately went into action.

"Now mayor, a bit ago the city settled a case and made some promises about access ramps." Jeremy began.

"Of course, yes, yes, I was greatly in favor of this and I have worked diligently to make this happen." The mayor said.

"Well, there are a number of places that need this

work done.

Here, here, and here. I have compiled a list of 20 well-traveled public areas that need work done." Jeremy sad

The mayor picked up one of the sheets of paper and glanced at it nonchalantly and then said, "I can't believe this, you have my word, and I am shocked to hear this. Thank you for bringing this to my attention."

The mayor stood up and motioned to the door while saying, "I want you to know that I will do my best to ensure that a plan is put in place to fix this problem. My secretary will give you a call. Now if there is anything else, I have another meeting..."

"This is not going away. You made promises to us and the city...you have already settled a number of other cases."

"Mr. Williams, all we can do is what we can do. Now my next meeting is right now and I am sure you understand that I need to go..."

Elliot stood up and smiled and said, "It is good to meet you mayor, I am sure we shall meet again." Elliot was already thinking through a plan."

The mayor shook his hand and said, "It was good meeting you, and it is good seeing you again." He said to Shereese.

Shereese, Jeremy, and Elliot walked out of the office and then walked out of the building.

"I am sorry, I thought he would be much more open to working with us."

Elliot smiled, "Don't worry, I will get him to work with us."

"And just how are you gonna do that El?" Jeremy said.

"Hold on." Elliot pulled his cell phone out of his pocket and dialed.

He called Kiona Booth the director at the nursing home. "Yes Sister Booth, I want you to get every resident that needs a wheelchair out on the street in front of the building in a wheelchair next Thursday at say 3PM."

"What? Why? Who is gonna...?"

"Sister Booth, I ain't got time to explain, but just do it."

He hung up.

"What are you up to El?" Jeremy said.

Elliot ignored him and asked Shereese, "Didn't you say we have a member of the church that works for Channel 16 news?"

Jeremy looked at him and said, "No El, No El...we need to do this the right way."

Shereese smiled and said, "Yeah Ariel Daniels. She is a reporter there.

Elliot smiled and asked, "Do you have her number?"

"No, Elliot, you ain't gonna do this." Jeremy said.

Shereese pulled out her phone and found Ariel's number and dialed.

"Ariel? The pastor wants to talk to you?" Shereese said. She then gave Elliot the phone.

"Sister Daniels, I am going to make this quick. The city has promised to work on handicapped accessible ramps off the city streets and the church's nursing facility has a number of residents who are hampered from using our facilities due to the city's inaction."

"Hmmm, let me get to working on a story." Ariel said.

"I have your story, in about an hour the handicapped residents of our facility will be all in the street attempting to use their wheelchairs to gain entry to our facility." Elliot said.

"Hmm…"

"You ever heard of a sit in?"

"Yes…"

"Well we are going to have a roll-in next Thursday at 3pm."

Ariel laughed. "OK, I will bring a camera man."

"Thank you, I will see you tomorrow then." Elliot said he hung up the phone and gave it to Shereese.

"See, I knew I shouldn't have gotten involved with you." Jeremy said while shaking his head. He left leaving Shereese and Elliot.

"OK, I have a protest to throw together. I need to get some other people here. Do you know any other place I can get some wheelchairs? Let's do a million chair march." Elliot said with a snicker.

"Do you think that is necessary?" Shereese smiled.

"Well, my ride just left, can you give me a ride back to the church?" Elliot asked Shereese.

They walked back to her car.

"I really don't know how to say this." Shereese broke the silence.

"Lawd." Elliot stopped and then looked at Shereese and said, "Just say it."

"David said that the LA church fell through and he now wants to be pastor of Bethel."

Elliot looked at her and said, "So why are you telling me this? You want me to step down?"

"No, I mean I just...I thought you should know." Shereese said while looking away from Elliot's eyes.

"So did David tell you to tell me?"

"No, he wanted to surprise you at the next ministerial meeting."

"Does Minister Aaron know?" Elliot asked.

"I didn't tell him."

Elliot smiled inwardly as he came to the conclusion that Shereese was looking out for his best interests.

"So is your man gonna be mad at you for telling me?" Elliot flashed a slight smile.

"I told you to stop calling him that."

"Well he is your man, right? Why are you seeking to mess up his plan by telling me?" Elliot asked.

"I'm just telling my pastor something I think he should know."

Elliot smiled.

Elliot thought about it for a moment and then realized he had a lot more important things to do then worry about David's attempts to take over the church.

"Well thank you Sister Harris for supporting your pastor. As for your man..."

Shereese frowned.

"...I got something up my sleeve for him. Now let's get back to the church so I can get to work." Elliot said.

***

Minister Aaron was making small talk with Elliot when Reverend David Michael rushed into the pastor's study.

"Sorry I'm a bit late." Michael said.

Elliot said, "I didn't even know you were coming."

David chuckle nervously and said, "Brother pastor, I need to make a surprise announcement today, if I can."

"What is this announcement regarding?" Elliot said. *The last thing I need is David Michael announcing that he wants my church.*

"I said it is a surprise."

"You can understand that neither Reverend Charles nor I trust you to do anything but act a fool, so you are going to have to tell us what this announcement is or we are not going to let it happen.

David threw up his hands, looked at Minister Aaron in his eyes and asked him, "So you are saying that I can't make any more announcements in church without your approval?"

"No, what both of us are saying is that you are not going to make any more announcements in this church without my approval." Elliot said.

"I wasn't talking to you." David said.

"I am the pastor."

"No, you are the interim pastor, and that is soon to change."

Elliot smiled and then said, "How bout this, I'm the closest thing to a pastor you got right now, so you are gonna tell us your announcement or it ain't gonna happen."

"I ain't trying to start no fight. This is a high day. I just want to take a moment to ask Shereese Harris to marry me."

The air left Elliot and Minister Aaron rolled his eyes.

David continued, "God has certainly blessed us and I think the time is right."

Elliot looked at Minister Aaron who stood there with his mouth open.

No one said anything.

"So what do you say pastor?"

Elliot didn't say anything for a few more seconds.

"Pastor?" Minister Aaron asked.

Elliot attempted to paste a smile on his face and said, "Sure, how about right before the sermon?"

"I have a song for the choir to sin, I have already told them about it."

"No song, no fanfare, do your proposal, and then we

will move on with the service." Elliot said.

"Now come on, this is Reverend Harris' church and this is a once in a lifetime moment."

Minister Aaron touched Elliot on the hand and said, "If I may interrupt, I don't want to step over any bounds, but I think it would be fine if you have one song and you have your moment. But Reverend, we are trusting that you will do right by us, the church, and Shereese."

Elliot shook his head in the affirmative.

David smiled and said, "Thank you Minister Aaron."

"Now that we have that out of the way, we need to talk about the rest of the service." Elliot said.

"Yes, what is this I hear about an event at the retirement facility?"

"What event?" David interrupted.

"Yes, yes, I am going to need to make a special appeal to the church to be out on Thursday afternoon."

"Folks are at work pastor, this is not a well thought out plan." David interrupted again.

"If people can't come, they can't come, if they can come, they will come. I just need as many as I can get there to send a message to the mayor…"

"A message to the mayor? The mayor has been good to this church, are you sure you want to anger him?" David interrupted yet again.

"Our people can't even get into our retirement facility, so I wonder how good the mayor has been to this church." Elliot said.

"The mayor gave a commendation to a member of this church just last year."

"The mayor gave you a commendation, I don't know how much good it did the church." Minister Aaron said.

"Gave you a commendation for what?" Elliot said.

"For being the head of our bookmobile for underprivileged youth." David said.

"What bookmobile?"

"Exactly, what bookmobile? There ain't no bookmobile. You want to know why, because he spent all the money on advertising himself." Minister Aaron said.

"How much money has this church spent on advertising Reverend David Michael's ministry?" Elliot asked.

"Too much." Minister Aaron said.

"It ain't like that. The little money that we have can no longer support the ministry."

"How about we take the money we use to put you on TV every week?" Elliot said.

"No, that is a proven ministry."

"A proven ministry that you should know I'm about to close down, starting this week."

"What!" David said in anger.

"We need to get into this later." Minister Aaron said.

"You are right Minister." Elliot said before continuing to talk about the service.

David eyed Elliot the whole time.

"Ok, let's go in." Elliot said as they walked into the sanctuary.

The service progressed as the spirit moved. Elliot had to admit to himself however that he was not looking forward to the proposal that was to come.

Throughout the service he would catch a glance of Shereese and attempt to look away. On occasion he could have sworn that she was returning his gaze.

They entered the announcement time. Minister Aaron told the church about the Thursday meeting at the retirement community. The people barely responded.

David leaned over to say to Elliot, "It looks like you may not have many." David smiled.

Elliot leaned over to David and asked, "Are you gonna be there?"

David sat back up as if he didn't hear the question.

It was then approaching the moment of truth. Elliot tapped David who was standing next to him and shook his head letting him know it was time.

David stood up to the pulpit and said, "The Bible says that he who has found a wife has found a good thing."

A soloist from the choir began to sing lightly in the background, "You are flesh of my flesh, bone of my bone..."

David continued speaking what turned out to be a sermonette that maybe went for twenty minutes.

However, Elliot kept glancing towards Shereese who returned the glance.

David finally finished his sermon and asked Shereese to come up.

Elliot tried to figure out how happy she was, if at all. Everybody at this point knew what was about to happen.

When Shereese got up to on the rostrum, David said, "Now, if your father were here, I would ask him for your hand, but because he is not here, I will ask his church. Bethel, may I ask her to by wife?"

Minister Aaron crossed his leg impatiently and stared at the event happening.

However, the congregation loudly shouted in the affirmative.

David smiled and went down on one knee and pulled a small box out of his pocket. He opened the box and showed it to Shereese and then said into the microphone, "Shereese Harris, will you marry me?"

Shereese looked shell shocked as a result of the whole affair.

There was a tense few moments before she finally said, "Yes."

The choir began singing an up tempo gospel song and David got from his knee. He put the ring on Shereese's finger and hugged her.

Minister Aaron just shook his head.

David then said, "So now I am going to get married to the most beautiful woman in the world. I also want to let you know that God has told me that I need to stay at Bethel, so I am not going to Los Angeles. We will stay here and build up this ministry that my father-in-law started."

Minister Aaron looked like he wanted to hit somebody at that point.

David continued. "I know we have a good interim pastor, but I wish to take this moment right here and right now to put my name in for consideration as the next pastor of this church."

Minister Aaron was about to jump from his seat, but Elliot shook his head no.

The congregation's jubilation was a bit tempered at that point, as many in the congregation stared at Elliot.

Then there were a few awkward moments before David finally said, "Thank you and God bless…"

He and Shereese walked off the rostrum and then out of the church.

Elliot then took the pulpit and started his sermon as if nothing had happened.

He preached about the men who took the lame man to Jesus and had to go through the room to get him to a healing.

As he entered the close of the sermon he said, "Now, my sisters and brothers, we have some people who cannot walk in our congregation."

"Yes Lord." Someone said.

"Well, this Thursday, I want to you to stand up with them just like the men stood up with the lame man in the Bible." Elliot Continued.

"Uh huh…" Someone shouted.

"You heard the announcement, and you may not have planned to be there, but God needs you to help somebody get to Jesus."

"Yes Lord."

"You may need to go to work, but God needs you to help somebody get to Jesus."

"Come on."

You may have other things to do but God needs you to help somebody get to Jesus."

"Yes…" Someone shouted.

"This Thursday, God needs you to help somebody to get to Jesus…Who is gonna be with me helping someone get to Jesus?"

About ten stood up.

"If you are gonna help somebody get to Jesus on Thursday with me, I need you to stand up with me right now. Who is going to be there?"

About twenty more stood up.

"Now that's what I'm talking about. We stand with those who can't stand."

More members stood up.

Elliot continued his sermon close as the people were especially energized by the preaching and the appeal.

***

Deacon Miller, Tanya Ward, Minister Aaron, and

Kiona Booth sat in the office for the weekly minister's meeting.

Elliot felt a tinge of ambivalence about the meeting. He knew it was not going to be pleasant. He also knew it had to be done. There was just no way that the church could continue paying for all of David Michael's side projects as well as get the work it needed done.

The group was chit chatting about the upcoming "roll-in." In addition they chatted about the savings that needed to be suggested to the full church trustees meeting for ratification.

David walked in and Minister Aaron rolled his eyes.

"I sure do look forward to the wedding." Deacon Miller said.

Elliot cringed inwardly as he thought about it. He was starting to grow a little attached to Shereese and he tried to forget the big proposal on Sunday morning.

David smiled. "I do too."

David sat down and said, "Shereese said she is going to be a bit late and told me to tell you to start, but before you do, I must let you all know something important."

"Go ahead." Elliot said.

"I am formally putting my name in for pastor of the church. I think Pastor Charles has done a good job, but we really need to move on before he makes some decisions that cannot be undone."

Elliot impatiently looked at David.

"OK, that's good to hear. Now on to our business."

Elliot said.

"I am not finished. I think we shouldn't make any decisions until the church votes on my candidacy for pastor. In light of the fact that the church desperately wanted me to be the pastor in the past, I think it makes sense that we assume that they will want me right now." David said.

So now he think he is the pastor? Elliot thought.

"Minister Aaron, who is the pastor right now?" Elliot asked.

"You are."

"Now come on, you don't really think the people are going to side with you. Ain't nobody wanting they pastor to be preaching from a toilet." David said.

"I would, and I have a building full of residents who agree." Kiona said.

David glared at her and asked Elliot, "Why is she even here?" He pointed at Kiona.

"I'm here because my pastor wanted me to talk about the needs of our facility." She said to David.

"The facility needs to be cut out. Why do we even continue to support it? It is falling apart." David said.

"She is here because we are going to fix that ministry." Elliot said.

"I heard about your proposed cuts to ministry. Real ministry. You are going to cut successful ministries to try to save broke down ministries that no longer are helping the community." David said.

Shereese walked in at that time and sat next to David.

"Now hold on David, my daddy started that ministry to aid our senior members in their transition to the next plane. He even stayed in it a few days before he left to be with the Lord." Shereese said.

"All, I'm saying is that you don't cut real ministry to support old dying ministries that no longer work."

"And just what kind of ministry is being done by your television show?" Minister Aaron asked.

David looked angry and then calmed down and said, "I'm glad you asked. Over the last three years we have 5 new members due to that show. We have 300 people on the mailing list. The shut-in residents tell me that they watch the show regularly."

"We have 45 residents at the retirement facility who would love to have that money." Kiona said.

"Hold on Kiona, Reverend Michael is so full of it. The church sends videos of the church service to the shut-in members." Minister Aaron said.

"So now you calling me a liar? I can give you the names and numbers of people right now."

"Do it!" Minister Aaron said.

David started rattling off a few names when Elliot interrupted him. "OK, that's it. Let's stop pussyfooting around this. We can't afford it."

"I have financiers who are paying for it."

"OK, then you won't mind us dropping our financial support. We will drop it right now."

"Naw, we have to take a vote on it." David said.

"If we keep that show, there will be some changes made. For example, I as the pastor, will be over it. I would love to make that show talk about what we are doing and not simply a preaching show."

"You ain't even got the authority to do what you trying to do. The trustees gave me the show, only the trustees can take the show away from me."

"You know what, there ain't gonna be no vote. There ain't gonna be no vote of the trustees. You have had your last show that Bethel pays for."

"You can't do that!" David yelled.

"I will call the television studio to let them know

"Now, on to salaries."

"What?" David said.

"If you ain't at the church you won't get paid that week. That goes for me and that goes for all other paid members." Elliot said.

"Why are all of these financial savings coming at my expense?" David asked.

"Because you are the only one getting paid for doing nothing in this church." Elliot said.

"Doing nothing. So this Johnny come lately is going to attack me and my ministry, the next thing you will do is attack my engagement."

Elliot frowned up for a moment. He actually would love to attack that engagement, but thought better of saying anything about it.

"Now let's not get personal." Deacon Miller said.

Elliot went on. "And with these cost savings we will pay for a few updates to the Retirement facility and the youth multipurpose center. We will make Reverend Harris' plan come into fruition.

"So that's it, you think you are just gonna throw Reverend Harris' name around and get the church with you. OK, go ahead and do whatever you think you gonna do, cause at the next church meeting, I will be named the pastor."

Elliot smiled and said, "I hate to sound redundant, but Minister Aaron, who is the pastor now?"

"You are." Minister Aaron answered energetically. Shereese chuckled.

"OK, that's all I have, I will inform the Trustees what I have done.

"Not for long." David said. He then got up and grabbed the paper that Elliot had passed out and rushed out. Shereese followed him out of the room.

Shereese sat in Elliot's office as they prepared for the upcoming "roll-in."

"This is a lot more involved than I originally thought." Elliot said.

Shereese smiled and said, "If you gonna do it, you need to do it right."

"What is that supposed to mean?" Elliot feigned a fake frown.

"It's supposed to me that you can't do everything on the spur of the moment as you like to do."

"Give me one example of that." Elliot joked.

"I'll give you three."

"This aughta be good." Elliot said as he stared at her.

"Exhibit number one, preaching in a toilet." Shereese laughed.

"OK...Elliot laughed."

"Exhibit number two, having church while cleaning up the old building. There was no planning at all."

Elliot shook his head to demonstrate agreement.

"Exhibit number three, taking my cereal instead of putting it in my cart." Shereese laughed.

Elliot looked at her and said, "I thought you forgot that."

"Exhibit number four..."Shereese said as she picked up a piece of paper and began reading another one of Elliot's indiscretions.

"Hold on, hold on...you said three." Elliot said as he grabbed for the paper.

They playfully wrestled as Elliot continued to reach for the paper when their eyes met.

Shereese was immediately struck by the tenderness that she saw as their eyes locked. It was as if time stood still.

"Shereese?" David Michael said as he walked into the room.

"Shereese immediately looked back at David and

David glared at Elliot.

"Am I interrupting something?" David said.

"No David." Shereese said.

"Let me rephrase, "What am I interrupting?"

"We were just planning the roll-in."

"I ask because it looks like you have your arms around my fiancé." David said.

"I ain't, no…" Elliot said.

"Calm down." Shereese said.

"And you taking his side. Is there something you need to tell me?"

"I don't think you should be working with him. In reality, I don't know why we are doing this thing anyway. I am soon to be pastor and then we can get to real ministry and not playing games." David said.

Elliot smiled and said. "Real ministry like spending all the church's money to promote you."

"I'm tired of you coming in here attacking my ministry."

"I've done more ministry in the little time I have been here then you have done in years." Elliot responded.

David rushed over to Elliot and took off his jacket and Elliot stood straight.

Shereese stood in between them and pushed David back, "Calm down, what has gotten into you?"

"Oh, so you taking his side? You done bought into this fool's mess too? I'm gonna show you…" He pointed at Shereese.

"...that this guy is nothing." David continued.

Elliot laughed, "Might as well, because you already showed that you are nothing..."

David pushed Shereese to the side and she tripped and yelled as she hit the ground.

David then threw a punch at Elliot and hit him on the jaw.

"My leg." Shereese yelled as David rushed over to her.

"Get your hands off me."

She attempted to stand up and then couldn't put any weight on her leg.

She sat down on a chair.

Elliot had gotten up and rushed over to try to help her.

"Get your hands off her."

"You better leave him alone." Shereese said.

She looked him dead in his eyes.

"I should call the cops on your for assault."

"Assault? You jumped into the fray." David said.

"OK, everybody let's calm down. Let's get you to the emergency room to have them check out your leg." Elliot said.

"I'll take my fiancé to the ER, we don't need any help from you." David said.

"No, I think Reverend Charles should take me, and I think you need to calm down."

David looked at her, then looked at Elliot. He looked

back at her and said, "Are you sure?"

"I don't even want to see you right now." Shereese said.

"Watch your back." David said.

"What's that supposed to mean?"

"It means that I have almost figured it out. And as soon as I do, it will be over."

Elliot just looked at him.

David then walked out of the room and said it again, "Watch your back."

"Are you all right? It looks like David got a good lick on you." Shereese asked Elliot.

Elliot ignored the question and asked, "Are you really going to marry him?"

"I don't know."

"You deserve so much better."

Shereese chuckled, "Let's just go to the ER."

Elliot got her to her car and drove over to the Emergency Room.

As they sat in silence for a bit she said. "No…"

"No, what no?" Elliot asked.

"You asked me if I was going to marry him. At one time, I thought he was everything, but now I am learning that I shouldn't settle."

Elliot smiled.

"A good friend of mine said that I deserved better." Shereese continued.

"Now tell me something about yourself. I mean

besides that you can preach and you like Flavor-Os." Shereese said. She then recognized that she knew so little about him.

Elliot looked straight ahead as if trying to find some words.

"OK, we are almost there, I will answer one question about my background that you don't know." Elliot said.

"Your resume shows that you have pastored in some pretty big churches before coming here. Why did you come here?"

Elliot appeared in thought and then said, "I have spent my whole life searching for something. A work to do. Some place to be. But now, I think I have found it."

"Found what?"

Elliot put his hand over on Shereese's and said, "I think I have found the place to be."

Shereese smiled and playfully jerked her hand back and said, "Keep your hands to yourself pastor."

She then looked at him with a spark in her eye.

Elliot smiled and said, "OK, here we are. Let me go get a wheelchair to get you in."

Elliot laughed and said, "It appears you are gonna really be ready for the roll-in."

Shereese smiled and said, "Get in there…"

Elliot walked into the hospital and emerged a few moments later pushing a wheelchair.

Chapter 24 - Shereese

"So what happened to your leg girl?" Rachel asked Shereese as she took a sip of her raspberry lemonade.

Shereese reached down and touched the brace.

Shereese thought for a moment and realized she didn't want to get into it. She said, "Oh it's just a sprain, nothing to worry about. What you gonna order?"

Rachel looked at her and asked, "How did you sprain your ankle?"

"I fell down." Shereese said as she put the menu down and waved for the waiter to come over.

"Something tells me that you hiding something, what happened?"

Realizing that Rachel wasn't gonna let it go, she said, "OK, he pushed me."

Shereese took a sip of her lemonade.

Rachel Griffith started coughing as the surprise of Shereese's words caused her to swallow in the wrong way.

"Are you alright?" The waiter asked as he got to the table.

"You are going to have to give us a few more minutes." Rachel said to him.

She caught her breath and then angrily said, "What do you mean he pushed you, who pushed you?"

This was exactly what Shereese didn't want to get into, but now she had to tell the whole story.

"David pushed me..." Shereese began to say.

"Hell naw..." Rachel blared.

"I got in the middle of a scuffle between him and Reverend Charles and he pushed me out of the way to get at him."

"So he didn't mean to?" Rachel asked.

"I'm sure he didn't, but girl you don't lose your temper like that. I didn't see Reverend Charles pushing nobody." Shereese said.

Rachel smiled and said. "Preachers fighting over you and whatnot."

"No, it wasn't like that."

"So what was it like?"

"Just David's jealous behind thinking something is going on between me and Elliot."

"Hmm...hmm. So it's Elliot now." Rachel said.

"What you trying to say?"

"I thought David was gonna be right for you, but you and I both know he is a loose cannon. Did he ask you to marry him because he scared he got competition now?" Rachel asked.

"I don't know, and I don't care, but I'm gonna call it

off. I don't need this." Shereese said.

Rachel smiled.

"What is it?" Shereese asked.

"I think you gonna need some counseling to get over your grief, you think Elliot will work you in for a pastoral visit?"

"Come on be serious."

"I am serious, you can't tell me that you ain't interested. And you know David does have something to worry about."

Shereese's phone buzzed.

"Let your answering machine pick it up. It's been a while since we had the chance to talk." Rachel said.

Shereese looked at her phone and saw it was Elliot.

"I really need to get this, it's David."

"We need to talk." Shereese said as she answered the phone.

"Can't you see that that preacher is trying to make the move on you?" David said.

"This ain't about him, this is about me and you."

"Come on, I apologized, you know I didn't mean it, don't you. I didn't mean to push you."

"I know you didn't mean to push me, I also know that you did. My foot is the same kinda hurt whether you meant to or not."

"Come on, God forgives. You are a preacher's daughter, you gonna forgive me or not?" David said.

"I forgive you, but this ain't working." Shereese said

into the phone.

Rachel was doing a happy dance with her hands at the table.

"What, because I accidentally bumped you?"

"You know it's more than that. You are always gone and you don't love me." Shereese said.

"What do you mean I don't love you?"

"When have you even said you loved me?"

"I love you babe. There. You happy. I love you. Who you been talking to putting all this stuff in your head? Is it Rachel, naw, I bet you it's that Minister Aaron."

"It's over."

"How you gonna do this on the phone?"

"I didn't know I was gonna do it, but it is done."

"So that's it, you leaving me for that preacher. He ain't going nowhere baby. I'm gonna make certain of that."

"What's that supposed to mean."

"I'm close, I'm gonna figure it out, and when I shoot him down, you and that fool are gonna go down together."

"Whatever…" Shereese said.

"Bye…" David yelled.

"Bye…" Rachel yelled and clicked off.

"Now that is what I'm talking bout." Rachel said.

Shereese felt a great calm come over herself. She knew she was doing the right thing.

The phone buzzed again.

"Who is it? Cause if it is David's trifling behind again,

I don't care whether he meant it or not you don't..." Rachel began to say.

"It's Elliot."

"Well like I said, this can wait, go head and answer that man." Rachel laughed.

"Hello pastor." Shereese said.

"Sorry to bother you, but I really need to talk to you about the wheelchairs. Did you talk to Sister Booth about getting that all together?" Elliot said on the phone.

"Didn't you say you were going to talk to her?"

"Oh, yes, that's right, well since I have you on the phone, I just wanted to make sure that your leg is healing nicely, I apologize again, and I should never have let it get to that point." Elliot said.

"It wasn't your fault. Although I was a bit surprised at your boxing skills." Shereese laughed and Elliot chuckled.

"Hey, since I got you on the phone, I thought we might have another meeting, you know to just go over the plans one more time." Elliot said.

Shereese smiled. "I agree, you can't go over the plans too many times."

"How about a couple hours before the roll-in. We can go over to the roll-in together."

"Ok, you heal up that leg, we are gonna need you."

"Just give me a wheelchair and I will be all right."

They laughed.

"It was good to talk to you. I really want you to know

how much I appreciate you. You are truly God sent."

"Bye…" Shereese said as she hung up.

"That sounds perfect pastor." Rachel mimicked Shereese.

"Shut up." Shereese playfully demanded.

Chapter 25 - Elliott

"You are going to have to hurry up Minister." Elliot told Minister Aaron as they both packed the Church van full of signs, wheelchairs, and other equipment that will be needed for the roll-in.

Minister Aaron looked at his watch and asked, "We got plenty of time, why you rushing me?"

Elliot said, "Shereese and I are going to meet before the meeting for lunch or something."

"Lunch or something?" Minister Aaron asked.

"Well, we thought it best that we discuss the final arrangements for the event."

"Just you two?"

"Well, yes…"

"Hmmm…" Minister Aaron said as he smiled.

He paused and then Minister Aaron said, "I would ask if I could come, but I probably would be in the way, don't you think?"

"Yes…" Elliot said trying to keep a straight face. Then they both laughed.

"Praise God, I have been praying that she would date

someone with sense. I hope this means that David Michael is out of the picture." Minister Aaron said.

"I don't know about Reverend Michael. All I know is we are going to discuss things."

"Well then why are you dragging your feet, let's finish packing this van so you can get out of here." Minister Aaron said as he helped Elliot put the last few things in the van.

Elliot hopped in the van a few minutes later and was about to drive off when Minister Aaron walked up to the window.

"You got my blessing." Minister Aaron said.

"Blessing for what?"

"You know what I'm talking about. I been praying on it, and I think that God may be answering that prayer."

Elliot smiled and said, "Keep praying."

He then drove off to Shereese's apartment to pick her up. Traffic was brutal and so he got there about an hour and a half before the roll-in was to begin.

He jumped out of the van and walked up to her apartment and the door flew open.

He knocked on the door and she quickly answered.

"Come in and sit down." She said. Elliot walked in.

She walked by with a slight limp.

Elliot shut the door and sat down.

"I got some leftover chili that you need to eat."

Elliot sat down.

She was still running around getting a few things

together.

"Come sit with me." Elliot said.

"I can't sit down if I'm gonna…"

"Come on for a few minutes."

She looked over at him and then said. "OK, just a few."

She walked over to him and sat in the chair immediately next to him at the table.

"I need to get something off my chest." Elliot said.

Shereese took a deep breath and sighed as she looked into his eyes.

He took her his right hand and told her. "David was right. I uh…" He began to say and then hesitated.

Shereese waited for a moment and asked, "You what?"

"I am interested in you, as you probably can tell. You are exactly what I have been waiting for. I know you are in a relationship but…"

"Well that's over…"

"Well, I want to do this right. How about I take you to dinner tonight, to celebrate the victory we are going to have today at the roll-in."

Shereese smiled and said, "That will be nice."

Shereese then said. "Now hurry up and eat so you can be there. Without you this will not work."

Elliot smiled and took a bite.

***

Elliot drove Shereese over to the retirement home and Shereese followed in her car. Traffic was extremely backed up and traffic was totally shut off to the street that the retirement community was on.

There were a lot of police officers directing traffic to side roads.

Elliot finally got there an hour late. He jumped out the van and saw a number of people standing around, including David standing with a megaphone. He obviously was trying to control the situation. Shereese jumped out and walked up next to Elliot.

"Can I talk to you...Alone?" David asked Elliot while looking at Shereese.

"Thank you for keeping the people here." Elliot said.

"I need these people here. We are about to make something very clear." David said.

"What are you talking about?" Elliot answered.

David leaned in and said. "Your event is done. The mayor blocked traffic for a parade, ain't nobody gonna get here."

"What parade?" Elliot asked.

"Some parade that the mayor and I cooked up to stop this mess you throwing down."

"What?" Elliot said.

"But that is the least of your worries Mr. Elliot James."

Elliot's eyes widened in shock.

"Yeah, that's right, I know who you are and these

people out here are about to know who you are."

"No, uh...Let's go over here and talk." Elliot said as the two walked to the side.

David had a huge grin on his face and followed Elliot over to the side.

Elliot's head was spinning.

"OK, you ain't Reverend Charles. You ain't Elliot Charles. You ain't Carl K. Charles. You are some guy named Elliot James and you have been perpetrating a lie on this community for months."

"You don't understand..."

"Oh I understand. You in here trying to be me. Trying to take my church. Trying to take my girl. Well you know what, all of that ends today."

"What do you want?"

"You still don't get it. It's over."

Elliot stood there in shock as David walked over to the front of the small group including the local news who had showed up for the event.

"It really pains me to say this, but our interim pastor is a scammer."

Minister Aaron yelled out, "What are you talking about?"

"He is not a pastor; he has never been a pastor."

There was grumblings in the crowd.

"You know who I talked to the other day? Pastor Carl K. Charles. He called me because he wanted to be considered for the position again. Imagine his surprise when I told him he was already the pastor."

Again there was groaning in the group.

"This man here is not Carl K. Charles he is some con man named Elliot James."

Shereese walked over to Elliot and asked him, "Is it true?"

Elliot dropped his head.

Shereese started crying and ran back to her car and began driving home.

There was yelling and anger in the crowd.

"If you don't believe me ask him." David said.

A group walked over to him and he just dropped his head.

"Give me the keys." David asked.

"The keys to what?"

"The keys to the church van, the church, and the Pastor's apartment. You don't think we are going to continue subsidizing you do you?" David said.

Elliot took out the keys and put them in his hand.

"How am I gonna get home?"

"What do I care?" David said.

Minister Aaron rushed up and took the megaphone from David.

"My sisters and brothers, we have a lot to digest. Please just go home and you will hear from us."

The newscaster was already talking to a few members of the church.

Elliot sat in the corner with his head down when

Minister Aaron walked up and asked, "You need a ride?"

Elliot still looking down said, "Yes."

"Come on."

A few members were shouting profanities at him as he walked to the car. He got in and Minister Aaron drove.

The traffic caused by the alleged parade really caused the traffic to back up. The tension in the car was very thick.

After about a half hour of silence Minister Aaron asked, "So what's your name?"

"Elliot James."

"What do you do?"

Elliot chuckled. "I am a student among other things."

Minister Aaron laughed.

"When I walked into the church I had every intention of applying for the secretary job, but then before I knew it I was applying for the pastor job."

Minister Aaron laughed again, "So that's where all that taking out the trash business came from."

Elliot said, "Right…"

"Well since you have been the pastor for these last few months, you know more than anybody that there was some trash that you needed to take out."

That broke the ice. They both laughed.

Minister Aaron made a turn down a back street and said, "Listen here. You did wrong. You shouldn't have perpetrated this lie for so long…"

"I know, I just…"

"Pastor, let me finish…" Minister Aaron said.

Elliot shut up and thought that this is probably the last time he would be called pastor.

"I am a good judge of character. And you did wrong, but I still know a pastor when I see one."

Elliot stared at him with a shocked look on his face.

He continued. "Now pastor, I think you probably need some training, but you been called. I know it. This church is not the same church it was when you came here."

Elliot sat quietly listening.

"The youth program is revitalized. We have a new building that we will use. Reverend Harris' plan is being implemented. And you know what?"

"What?" Elliot asked sheepishly.

"We are on the road to a financial stability that we haven't had since Reverend Harris died. You did wrong, but you keep your head up."

"Looking at the congregation, it looked like they may not agree. Sister Wilson looked like she wanted to take a switch to me." Elliot said.

"Well you lied to them, give them a bit of time to calm down and they will be loving you again."

"I don't think I am gonna come back to the church." Elliot said.

"What, never?"

"It's probably best that I don't come back."

"I disagree, like it or not, you are the pastor of this church until we elect a new one."

"You have got to be kidding…" Elliot said.

"You can't run from this church and you can't run from your calling."

It got quiet. And a few minutes later they drove up to the church.

"Remember what I said. You are still the pastor of this church."

"You think Shereese believes that?" Elliot asked.

There was silence. "You are gonna have to ask her yourself."

Elliot got out of the car and walked towards his car that was in the parking lot.

Minister Aaron yelled out his window. "You better keep in touch Pastor James."

It was the first time anyone had ever called him pastor with his real name. As Minister Aaron drove off, Elliot broke down and started crying as he got to his car. He got in.

Elliot picked up his cell phone and called Shereese. The phone rang a few times and then the answering machine picked up. "I cannot take your call right now, please leave your name number and a message."

Elliot began to speak, "Shereese…I…" And then he stuttered.

He then said, "I'm sorry." And hung up.

**

True to his word, Elliot didn't go back to Bethel. He called Minister Aaron periodically, but found it more and more difficult to talk to him. Minister Aaron again was the interim pastor and again he was hoping that someone would come pastor the flock.

Elliot found a small studio.

Jeremy walked into his apartment.

"Wow, you really are keeping this place up. I'm surprised." Jeremy said as he saw just a few dishes and a few magazines on the table.

Elliot laughed.

"So how's work?"

"Dennis is talking about promoting me into management."

"Wow man. You are a lot different than you were back when you lived with me."

"Yeah, I now. Ever since pastoring that church. My whole view of things have changed."

"By the way, you ever hear from them? I mean it has been what, two months?"

"Five months, two weeks…and three days. I used to hear from Minister Aaron, but it just got so hard to talk to him. I wanted to be there so bad."

"Well then why don't' you go back?"

"I don't know man…it would be so weird."

"You ever heard from Shereese?"

Elliot sat quiet for a moment and then said, "No, I tried to call her a few times and went straight to her answering machine. I really can't blame her. I can't blame anybody for being mad at me."

"Well, that church changed you, anybody can see it."

"Speaking of which, I think I'm gonna apply for seminary."

"What, more schooling?" Jeremy joked.

"Yeah, more schooling."

"Naw, I'm joking man, I think it is a good thing. You found your calling and it ain't helping women find their shoes at Dennis' store."

Elliot smiled, "Now ain't nothing wrong with selling shoes."

"Ain't nothing wrong with selling shoes, but there is something wrong with YOU selling shoes." Jeremy answered.

"I am going to need a reference, you think you could give me one?"

"You know it."

"So you going to the religious school in town?"

"No, I'm trying to apply to a school in Atlanta."

"Atlanta? So you moving on me?" Jeremy said.

Elliot smiled. "Yeah, you gonna finally be rid of me."

Jeremy laughed. "So as soon as you straighten up, now you leave. I still think you owe me about three grand."

"Yeah, I been meaning to talk to you about that three grand..." Elliot smiled

"Talk about what?"

"Well since I'm gonna become a preacher, I doubt I will be able to get you that anytime soon."

"Now that is the Elliot I know."

The two talked for a few more hours before Jeremy left.

***

A couple weeks later Elliot was in the grocery store looking down the cereal aisle and he caught a glimpse of Shereese reaching to get ahold of the Flavor-O's.

At first he thought about walking by. He figured she didn't really want to see him. The last time he had tried to call her, she let it go straight to her answering machine.

It had been months since the last time they talked, or even saw each other.

Elliot walked down the aisle and said, "So you are still eating that crap?"

Shereese looked back over her shoulder and then smiled, "Elliot."

She hugged him. "It has been months."

"Let me get that for you." Elliot reached up and then threw it into his cart.

"Oh now you didn't." Shereese joked as she playfully punched him.

He grabbed the cereal out of his basket and put it in hers.

"So how have you been?" Shereese asked.

"For real, or are you just making polite conversation?"

"No, I wondered what happened to you, I did mean to call you but you know it was so messed up."

"Yeah, I know I messed up, I don't blame you."

"You talk to anybody at the church?"

"Minister Aaron calls periodically, but you know not really."

"Well they miss you. Your name comes up every Sunday. Some wanted to vote you in as the permanent pastor."

Elliot smiled, "Well, I been meaning to come back, but I wondered if anybody wants to see me."

"Oh they want to see you. You ought to come back this Sunday. You are still the pastor."

"So you still haven't elected anybody?"

"Well David's name is up this Sunday."

"Wow, so are you two still..." Elliot began to ask.

"Oh no, we never got back together, in fact he is already dating Tanya Ward, the new treasurer, and they are the new hot item."

"So then, are you dating anyone?" Elliot asked.

He then immediately said, "Now that is none of my business, I shouldn't have asked, I'm sorry."

There was a moment of awkwardness and Shereese

said, "So you never answered, what's going on with you, for real."

"Well, I'm selling shoes."

"So how is that going for you?"

"It actually is going well, but I'm about to go to the seminary and study ministry in Atlanta."

Shereese looked surprised. "For real? Poppi will be happy to hear that."

"You know who should be pastor of the church?" Elliot said.

"Who?"

"Minister Aaron...your Poppi."

"Yeah, I know, but he ain't gonna take it.

"I'm gonna ask him for a reference. In fact I'm about to go move to Atlanta. I got a flight to Atlanta on Sunday."

"Sunday, wow. Why don't you go to the seminary in town?" Shereese asked.

"I don't know, I just thought it might be best to get out of town."

"I really did enjoy being with you...as pastor, I mean. Mom still says that you were the closest thing to Daddy she has ever seen."

"Now that is a big compliment, didn't she love David though?"

"Well she did, but now that David has revealed his plans to turn the youth center into a television studio and..."

"What?"

"Yeah, that fool is going to turn everything back to the way it was. He is going to eliminate Daddy's plan that you started to implement."

"And the members are all right with that?"

"I guess. It really looks like he could win the vote of the congregation."

"How does that make you feel?" Elliot asked.

Shereese laughed. "I will probably leave Bethel if he becomes pastor."

"You gonna fight?"

"Hard to fight by myself. Mom doesn't want to fight. Poppi, is tired of fighting. You left..."

Elliot looked at her.

"Nobody is gonna listen to me."

"Right. Well it has been good talking to you, take care." Shereese said.

She hugged him and walked away.

***

While standing in the grocery store, Elliot remembered the conversation he had with Minister Aaron a while back.

Elliot dialed him up on his cell phone.

"Pastor James." Minister Aaron said.

"Minister, I heard that the church is going to vote on Reverend Michael's name for pastor."

"You heard right. And it looks like he may win."

"Now, it seems that I remember you saying that the pastor can't name his successor."

"That's right."

Elliot continued, "But the pastor can eliminate from contention any one name."

Minister Aaron started laughing. "That is true."

"Am I still the pastor?"

"You are the pastor until the next pastor is elected."

"So if I wanted to eliminate David Michael's name from consideration, then I would be well within my rights as the current pastor of the church."

"That is true. Only you must do it in a duly called business session of the church."

"OK, one final question, When is the next church business meeting?"

"This Sunday when we will vote on the name of David Michael."

"Well, it is going to cut it close, I have a flight to Atlanta on that day, but I will be there on Sunday."

"You got business in Atlanta?" Minister Aaron asked.

"That's my second point. I'm going to go to Atlanta to the seminary."

"Seminary. Well praise God, I knew you were going to be a preacher. Why don't you go to seminary here though and come back to Bethel? We can make you an associate."

"Thanks, but I really need to leave town. I just wanted

to know if you would write me a reference letter."

"Yes sir, but still won't you consider the local seminary?"

"I'm sorry, but my mind is made up. But I will be there on Sunday. We simply cannot let David kill this ministry."

"I will see you Sunday." Minister Aaron said.

Chapter 26 - Shereese

"Well, this is the day." Shereese said to her mother as they sat in church in their regular seats.

"I guess if David is elected in we will have to move." Mother Harris said.

"If David is elected today, this is the last time I set foot in this church."

"Shereese, keep your voice down." Mother Harris said while looking around. "We are in church and others can hear you.

"Mom, I'm only here to vote against him. Otherwise I wouldn't even be able to listen to him."

"Just be quiet." Mother Harris said as a tear fell down her cheek. Shereese put her arm around her. It was definitely the end of an era.

Shereese remember sitting in that same spot when her father began preaching in that church. And the growth of the church. And now, it was all to end.

Minister Aaron and David walked out onto the platform.

The choir began to sing an upbeat song that got the

congregation involved. It felt almost like a coronation.

The worship service would have been moving except Shereese would not let herself be moved.

Then it was time for the preaching of the gospel. Minister Aaron stood up and said from the rostrum, "Well my sisters and brothers, today we will have the trial sermon by Reverend David Michael. After the sermon, we will vote on his candidacy to become pastor of this church."

David grinned deviously and stood up. "Thank you Minister."

"It has been a long time coming." David said.

Someone responded in the affirmative.

"I had plans to go somewhere else, but God had other plans. And now I and my dear fiancé Sister Tanya Ward look forward to pastoring this church."

"Uh huh." Someone said.

Shereese rolled her eyes.

"We look forward to being here a long time."

"Until something better comes along." Shereese whispered into her mother's ears.

"Shhh..." Mother Harris said.

"But before we begin I must tell you what God told me we need to do at this church."

Then David began to outline his plan of more media ministry, attempts to turn the church into a mega church, and more programs to appeal to young adults.

Shereese noted that there was nothing about the

youth or senior citizens.

"I hope people can see through his mess." Shereese whispered to her mother a little louder. Someone in the pew behind them chuckled.

Mother Harris ignored her daughter.

The sermon then ended with a whoop that brought the people to ecstasy. The congregation seemed to be willing to do whatever David wanted at that point.

After the sermon he called Tanya up with him and they stood there together.

Then Minister Aaron stood up and said, "OK, before we can vote on the next pastor, I think it is fitting and correct that the current pastor of the church says something."

Shereese smiled and looked around as Elliot walked confidently to the pulpit.

"What kind of scam are you running Aaron?" David yelled.

Elliot walked up to the microphone.

Minister Aaron gave Elliot a piece of paper. Elliot took the paper and put it in his jacket inside pocket.

"I am the pastor of this church right now." Elliot yelled.

"Boo...Boo. No." Were peppered throughout the congregation. But then there was some cheers.

"Listen to him." Shereese yelled along with a few others.

"As pastor of this church, I do not have the ability to

name my successor, but I can eliminate one name from contention."

"What!" David yelled. "What is he talking about?" David continued.

"So I wish to eliminate David Michael from consideration as pastor, he is not fit for the title of pastor of this church."

"What…"

Mother Harris leaned over to Shereese and said, "I remember when your father put that into the bylaws."

David grabbed the microphone and said, "This guy was never the pastor, he was interim pastor."

"He was duly elected as interim pastor, the bylaws do not distinguish between interim senior pastor and senior pastor."

"Well, it should."

There was a lot of noise in the congregation at this point.

Elliot took the microphone back and said, "You have had the best pastor you ever will have in Minister Aaron, I strongly suggest that you name him pastor."

"No, I'm gonna kick your…" David yelled as his profanity was drowned in the noise of the congregation.

"I loved being your pastor and I really believe that this is the best thing I could do for the church." Elliot said.

"I got a plane to catch. So I wish you all well." Elliot said as he rushed out of the room.

Shereese rushed up to the front of the auditorium and said, "I agree, can I make a motion to vote Minister Aaron as the next pastor of Bethel."

"You are out of order. Somebody get her off the mic." David yelled.

"Sisters and brothers, please, calm down, please calm down." Minister Aaron said.

After a few moments order was restored in the congregation.

David then said, "OK, now vote on my name."

"Your name cannot be voted on according to the bylaws."

"I'm gonna sue you." David pointed at Minister Aaron.

"I'm gonna sue that fake preacher Elliot whatever his name is. I'm gonna sue Bethel." David then looked at Shereese and said, "I'm gonna sue you too."

Shereese laughed.

David then took Tanya's hand and they walked out of the building.

A few other people left with him, but the rest of the congregation sat there waiting.

"As to your suggestion Shereese, I am not qualified to pastor this church."

"You have pastored this church without the title for many years, I think it is time you took the title."

"So move." Someone yelled from the audience.

"You move what?" Minister Aaron said.

"I move that you be the pastor."

"Second." Someone else yelled.

"I ain't called for the second."

Shereese smiled and said, "Well then call for it."

"Normally, you aren't allowed to chair a meeting that votes on your name."

"Well desperate times call for desperate measures." Shereese said with a smile.

"Ok, is there a second?" Minister Aaron said.

Someone yelled "Second."

"All in favor note by saying aye."

The vast majority of the congregation said "Aye."

"And opposed say nay."

A few said nay. And Minister Aaron said. The Ayes have it, I guess you just elected me as pastor of the church.

"Do you know Elliot's flight? I kind of want to…"

"If you hurry you might catch him. He is traveling to Atlanta." Minister Aaron smiled. "It is North American Flight 7856."

Chapter 27 - Shereese

Shereese rushed to the airport, but she was not sure what she was going to do when she got there. She wanted to make it clear though, that she was open to a relationship.

As she drove up to the short term parking, she jumped out of her car. Walking right by the sign that read, "Any unattended vehicles will be towed." She didn't care at that point.

She rushed in and looked up at the board that read flight 7856 was boarding. She knew she couldn't get to the flight in time so she ran to a ticket agent for North American flights.

There was a line of people looking impatiently as she jumped the line.

"I need to give a message to one of your customers boarding flight 7856," Shereese said.

"We can't do that, it's against company policy unless it is an emergency. And besides, there is a long line in front of you." The middle aged black woman said.

The young black woman customer who was standing

at the gate asked Shereese, "Why do you need to send a message?"

"I need to answer his question." Shereese responded.

The young customer said, "His? Is this business or personal."

The middle aged woman looked at her and said, "Yeah, is this business or personal."

"Well, um, it's kinda." Shereese began to stammer.

"OK, please get in line Ms." The ticket agent said.

"I need to stop my man before he leaves."

"Go head and let her send the message, sounds like an emergency to me." The young customer said with a smile.

The person next in line said, "Yeah, send the message."

Then a few others took chimed in. Shereese looked around and smiled.

The ticket agent looked at her again and smiled and said, "If you say it's an emergency, it's an emergency. What customer and what message."

"To Elliot James, from Shereese Harris, message is 'I need to answer your question before you leave. Call me on my cell at 765-9311.'"

The ticket agent picked up a phone and called the message over.

"Thank you."

Shereese said to both the agent and the customer. She then began walking to the gate knowing she wouldn't get there in time.

Her phone didn't ring.

She scrambled to the gate not knowing what she would say or what she would do, but hoping to see Elliot.

When she got to the departure gate the door was closed and the plane was gone.

She looked up at the big screen and saw that the flight had departed on time.

She fell into one of the seats that was still warm from waiting customers and thought about the times she had had.

She remembered her first interaction with Elliot at the grocery store. She remembered how he worked hard for the church and others.

As her mind was traversing these times, her phone rang.

She looked at it and saw it was Elliot.

She picked up almost immediately and jumped up, "Hello."

"You said you have to answer my question."

"The answer is no…" She quickly answered.

"No? What question is that?" He asked.

"You asked me was I seeing someone. I never answered the question. The answer is no."

Elliot hung up.

Shereese yelled, "Hello…Hello…We got cut off."

Elliot laughed. He was standing right behind her. He said, "So the answer is no. Well we are going to have to change that aren't we?"

She smiled and rushed towards him and hugged him. And then they kissed.

Epilogue

Six Months Later.

The open window dominated the small studio apartment. Elliot James, laid on the couch with a theology textbook in his hand and an open laptop on the table in front of him. Elliot was wearing some business casual slacks.

The collar was open on his white dress shirt and his necktie was loosened. The fingers of Elliot's right hand barely touched the textbook. His head was turned to the left side as he snored while lying across the sofa. Next to Elliot was a number of Bibles in different translations and languages.

Shereese Harris opened the door with her key that Elliot had just given to her since their relationship was so strong. He wanted her to have a key to his apartment.

Shereese saw Elliot lying there and yelled, "What are you doing! Come on we have a meeting at the church." Shereese yelled, "Eliot...Eliot...Get up!"

Elliot jumped which caused the books to fall all over the place.

"See this is why I should be through with you."

"Come on babe, I was just studying, I need to get this paper done." Elliot said as he picked up a book.

Shereese walked over to the refrigerator and saw it was empty. "What am I going to do with you? You don't have anything. I was hoping to get a sandwich or something before we go."

She looked up in the cabinet. "What is this you don't even have any Flavor-Os. What's the matter with you?"

"Well there is Shredded Wheat." Elliot said and laughed.

She walked over to him and said, "I ain't playing with you."

"Well, I want to play with you. He said as he put his arms around her and kissed her."

***

Did you enjoy this book? Here is a sneak peek preview of Book 1 of our Living Praise Series available now. Purchase here.

Sneak Peak – Living Praise Book 1

"Lord, I call your name."

Sweat traversed Tommy Settle's forehead as he strained to produce the high notes he sang on the album so many years ago.

After he failed, Tommy flashed his sparkling smile at the one thousand who came to attend Living Praise's last American concert before their European Tour.

Tommy strained for another note. He missed it. Someone in the crowd gasped.

"Bring it to a close Tommy." Mary Hill, the thirty-nine year old childhood buddy of Tommy, whispered. "It ain't working," she continued.

Tommy looked toward Mary and then away. He started prancing around as he missed yet another note on the song he made famous years before.

Mary rolled her eyes.

Tommy attempted a musical run that failed.

The other seven singers of Living Praise stole glances at each other. They tried to hide Tommy's mistakes by increasing the volume of their background vocals, but the Holy Ghost left the room.

Mary stomped and clapped like you see in the small Pentecostal churches in an attempt to save the mood of the concert.

"Yes, Lord." Mary said to the other members of Living Praise.

Carol Mace, the petite beautiful, dark-skinned soprano, grabbed her microphone. She hit a note so high and powerful that the audience had no choice but to respond with praise.

Tommy stopped prancing long enough to straighten his body up to its full 6 feet 5 inch frame. He looked at Carol, letting her see the anger written all over his face, but she continued to sing.

Lester King, the middle aged bass of the group, boomed a part. Tommy jumped, not expecting it at that point. Although showing signs of weakening, Lester's deep bass could still cause the women to melt and the men to be mesmerized.

Tina Cage and Ricky Dean, the background singers who were not full-fledged members yet, sang strongly, providing support.

David Small, powerful lean and fine lead singer on most of the group's latest hits, added his voice to Tommy's. The women shouted every time he touched the microphone.

Tommy attempted to sing over David, but there was no contest.

"I call, I call, I call." David supported the melody. He hit a few notes that Tommy missed moments earlier.

Tommy's brown-skinned face got beat red as his temperature rose.

Anyone could see the anger brewing in Tommy. And Tommy kept on pushing. He kept on trying to sing.

The band director, Dennis Terrance, raised his hand to slow the music down and end the show.

During the close, Mary walked over to Dennis and said something.

Tommy stared in the air as anger and surprise came on him. The show should be ending. They always ended with "I Call Your Name."

Mary walked back to the group. She leaned in to speak to the group. "We ain't gonna end like that. David, I want you to bring us home with 'Power to Live.'"

Tommy sneered at Mary, "We already sang that song, why are we going to sing 'Power to Live' again?"

Mary turned and raised her index finger and pointed straight at Tommy and said, "Listen here,

Tommy. What happened to your voice? When are you gonna do something about it?"

David said, "It ain't time for this now, let's sing the song and talk about this later."

Mary said, "You right, take it from the top."

David sauntered up to the mic.

The crowd yelled.

"Sing it, David," someone in the audience yelled.

David yelled in the mic, "How many of you need power to live?"

The people yelled in unison, "Yeaaahhhhh."

"Is anybody in here? Somebody said y'all worship in Nashville, so I'm gonna ask again. How many of you need some power to live?"

The response from the crowd was so loud it about brought the roof off the place.

David looked back at Mary and asked said in the microphone, "Mary?"

Mary yelled back in a sassy tone, "What you want David?"

"We sang it before, but do you think they want us to sing it again?"

Many in the crowd yelled, "Yes! Yes, David!"

The heat rose in Tommy's head. He was about to blow his top.

David pointed to Dennis Terrance, who led the band to the first few notes of "Power to Live."

David effortlessly sang the notes and the people rocked to the music.

This was their last big hit. "Power to Live" had been on the gospel charts for four weeks the year before. The song became a fan favorite. What was special about this song is that all three of the lead singers in the group took a turn at the lead.

Carol Mace, the powerful soprano, came in right on key and took the song to another level. Everybody could feel the music flowing and the song moving forward.

David and Carol sang off each other in a way that brought more and more of the audience to their feet singing and praising God.

The soulful tenor of David blended with Carol to create a tension that drove the audience wild with anticipation of what was next.

It was time for Tommy to come in and take a lead. Tommy looked at David, shook his head, and sang. Tommy split a couple notes and creaked. Tommy felt his voice leaving and started preaching.

"I tell ya, I need some power to live. I need power to grow. I need that power. Is anybody in here that needs that power?" Tommy yelled as he attempted to recover from the problematic singing.

However, his preaching routine didn't go over well. The rest of the group started cutting evil glances at Tommy.

Mary whispered, "Get off the mic, Tommy."

Tommy ignored her and kept on speaking. He started preaching a medley of sermonic closes he had gathered from multiple television preachers.

"Get off the mic, Tommy!" Mary said.

Tommy continued his show-killing antics.

Mary got the sound engineer's attention and did the universal sign to cut off someone's mic by running her index finger across her neck.

Tommy's mic shut off and stopped.

David eased back in to attempt to salvage the song.

Tommy continued to talk, but his microphone was dead. He continued to preach for a bit before he realized what had happened.

Carol and David continued their singing to finish the song. The audience, however, sensing something was wrong, were paralyzed.

Tommy, realizing that his microphone was dead, threw it on the ground and walked over to the sound engineer who had cut his mic and started yelling at him.

"What was that man?" Tommy yelled.

"It's over, Tommy. Calm down and finish the song."

"So now you telling me what to do? Who are you to tell me anything?"

"Please let me do my job. Now go back out on stage or go back to the dressing room. I don't care what you do, just leave me alone," the engineer said.

Tommy walked to the side of the stage where he could still see what was going on.

A tear emerged in Tommy's eye as he recognized he had let his anger get the best of him again. Tommy saw the rest of the group work together like a well-oiled machine without him. Even his part was taken over by Ricky.

Tommy wouldn't admit it to anyone, but the group sounded much better than it ever had. Even ten years before when he, Mary, Devon, George, and Shereese, the original Living Praise, started singing praises to God in much smaller venues than this church auditorium.

Now after ten years of singing, he wondered why everything was falling apart. He wondered why his voice was starting to betray him.

Ten years ago, Tommy could hit any note at any time. He "wrecked the house" better than anyone else, but now, the group he and Mary started was slipping out of his hands.

Tommy was not featured on any songs on their last CD. In addition, he didn't even sing background on their last two songs, which featured either David, and/or Carol. On top of it all his voice was starting to leave him.

David hit his characteristic close to the song "Power to Live," which informed Tommy that the end of the song was near. Tommy rushed to the dressing room so he could meet them in there

Tommy often depended on Mary's loving and God-fearing nature to forgive him of his indiscretions, but deep within he knew that the day was coming when she would cease putting up with his shenanigans.

Mary was longsuffering, but when it came to Living Praise, she wouldn't let anybody mess the group up.

Tommy had just enough time to walk in the door before the rest of the group got there.

"What in the world was-" Mary said as she was the first one to open the door seeing Tommy taking off his jacket.

Mary calmed herself.

"Lord, help me deal with this knucklehead," Mary prayed out loud.

"Stop the dramatics, I should be mad at you, you cut off my mic while I was singing."

"Were you there? You were killing the Spirit."

"Killing the Spirit? So what are you saying, 'cause I missed a couple notes--?"

"Come on, Tommy, you started messing up. Then you gonna start preaching some nonsense?" Carol said.

"The Holy Ghost hit me and I had to do what the Holy Ghost says. I preached the Word. They call me 'Minister Tommy Settles' because I am a preacher."

"It was a spirit all right, but it wasn't holy," Mary said. The rest of the group sat quietly.

"Tommy, we trying to make sure the Lord is in the place," David said, breaking the silence.

"Don't talk to me, David. I ain't talking to you."

"What are you talking about?"

"Shut up before I shut you up."

"I wish you would, Tommy." David emphasized his name.

Tommy walked over to David, intending to hit him.

Mary stepped in between them and pushed Tommy.

"You messing up, and instead of taking it like a man, you back here trying to blame somebody else. I shut your mic off because you didn't sound like Living Praise. You sounded like amateur hour."

"Hold on, amateur hour? This group's first hit was propelled by my voice. I sang 'I Call Your Name.'" Tommy pounded his chest. "This group was put on the map by my voice. This is my group, if you keep messing up, I'm gonna shut your mic off," Tommy said to Mary.

Lester, the bass singer, stood up and said, "Tommy, I think you better shut up before you say something you can't take back."

"No, let him talk," Mary said, crossing her arms.

"What happened to you, Mary? Do you remember what I did for this group?" Tommy said.

"Shut up, Tommy." Lester's voice boomed in his bass.

"Done for the group? OK, I'm done." Mary answered. "Do you realize the situation we are in? Power Records dropped us. We no longer have a recording contract."

"And whose fault is that?" Tommy interrupted.

"Tommy...Yeah you founded the group with me. And yes, your voice brought us our first hit, but if you can't be a part of the group, then I will kick you out of this group."

"How you gonna do that? I have as much right to this group as you do. We started this group together."

"How am I gonna do that? The same way I kicked Devon out the group because he didn't want to sing backup. The same way I kicked George out the group. The same way--" Mary said.

"Sounds like we need to kick you out the group," Tommy interrupted.

Lester grabbed Tommy and walked him out the room.

Mary continued yelling while the two left the room.

Outside the room, Tommy heard Mary yelling, "I'm done with him and his attitude."

"Are you are listening to Mary?" Lester asked.

"She ain't kicking me out the group."

"Tommy, now you and I both know that she can. And the way you acting, she probably should."

"I think I'm gonna start my own group, and do it my way. I am so sick of Mary and her mess. Come with me, man. You, me, Carol, let's do it."

Lester laughed. "You are not so delusional to believe that anybody wants to join a group led by you. Yeah, you ain't old, but your voice is shot and you got a bad attitude. You need to hold on to this gig because ain't nobody want to hear Tommy Settles now."

Tommy was floored by Lester's statement.

"Come on, man, you know this," Lester continued. "Now you are gonna go back into that room and apologize."

"Apologize for what?"

"Apologize for show boating. Apologize for not being a good part of the team. Apologize for disrespecting Mary. Apologize to David--"

Tommy interrupted Lester. "I ain't apologizing to that pretty boy. Talk about show boating. But...I'll apologize to Mary."

Tommy and Lester walked back into the room. It was quiet at that time.

"Mary...Mary..."

Mary began walking out.

"Mary."

"What do you want, Tommy?"

"You were right. I was just having a bad night. I apologize..."

"Whatever."

"You know I love you, Mary."

"I love you too, Tommy, but this can't continue. You better get your stuff together and quick."

Tommy looked away as Mary walked out of the room. "And Carol, I didn't mean to mess with you or the group."

"I know, Tommy," Carol said as she rolled her eyes.

David cleared his throat.

Tommy didn't want to, but he did feel as though he should apologize to David along with everyone else. "Dave, I'm sorry. I don't want to fight you. Lester is too old to carry your behind out of here after I laid you out." Tommy knew the joke was pretty lame as soon as it left his lips.

David gave a quick laugh and said, "I hear you." He walked out.

"One big happy family," Lester said as he and the rest of the group walked out of the room.

DISCUSSION QUESTIONS

1) Who transformed more? Elliot, Minister Aaron, or Shereese?
2) Should Elliot have been given another chance to be the pastor of Bethel?
3) Since Elliot was changed by his interaction with Bethel, was it God's plan that he lie to get the job?
4) Did God call Elliot to be pastor of Bethel? Why or Why not?
5) Would you have voted for Elliot to be the pastor of the church?
6) Did Elliot make the right decision choosing the youth ministry over media ministry? Why or why not?
7) Why was Bethel enamored with David?
8) Was Elliot right when he said that all church folks want is a reason to shout in church?

***

Sign up by clicking here to be notified when Sherman Cox releases any more books.

CPSIA information can be obtained
at www.ICGtesting.com
Printed in the USA
LVOW10s2341240117
522075LV00001B/98/P